4 -

03

Sait Faik Abasıyanık

A Useless Man

SELECTED STORIES

▪   ▪   ▪

Translated from the Turkish by Maureen Freely and Alexander Dawe

archipelago books

Archipelago Books
232 3rd Street #A111
Brooklyn, NY 11215
www.archipelagobooks.org

Distributed by Random House
www.randomhouse.com

Library of Congress Cataloging-in-Publication Data
Sait Faik, 1906-1954.
[Short stories. Selections. English]
A useless man : selected stories / Sait Faik Abasiyanik ;
translated from the Turkish by Maureen Freely and Alexander Dawe. –
First Archipelago Books edition.
pages cm
Includes bibliographical references and index.
ISBN 978-0-914671-07-7 (alk. paper)
I. Sait Faik, 1906-1954–Translations into English. I. Freely, Maureen,
1952- translator. II. Dawe, Alexander, translator. III. Title.
PL248.S288A2 2014
894'.3533–dc23   2014030520

Cover art: Abidin Dino

Archipelago gratefully acknowledges the generous support from the
Turkish Cultural Foundation, the American Turkish Society, the Ministry of Culture and
Tourism through the TEDA Program, Lannan Foundation, NYC's Department
of Cultural Affairs, the National Endowment for the Arts, and
the New York State Council on the Arts, a state agency.

PRINTED IN THE UNITED STATES OF AMERICA

A Useless Man

SELECTED STORIES

· · ·

The Samovar

. . .

"That's the morning call to prayer, my son. Wake up or you'll be late for work."

Ali had finally found a job. He'd been going to the factory for a week. His mother was happy. She knelt down on her prayer rug and said her prayers. Entering her son's room with the Supreme Being in her heart, and seeing his dream rippling along his smooth face and long, supple form – a parade of machines, electric batteries, and light bulbs, a purr of oiled metal and diesel motors – she'd been reluctant to rouse him. Ali was as flushed and damp as if he'd just come home from work.

As it rose out of the mist, the chimney of the Halıcıoğlu factory seemed to crane its neck, like a rooster. How proud it looked as it gazed out at the first glimmers of dawn on the shores of Kağıthane. Any moment now, they'd hear the whistle.

At last Ali woke up. He embraced his mother. He pulled his quilt over his head, as he did every morning, leaving his feet unprotected. His mother bent down to tickle them. Her son jumped up, and when she fell back onto the bed with him, giggling like a girl, she could count herself as happy.

There weren't many who could say that. Was it not the very modesty of their existence that lit their souls? What could a mother wish from a child, or a child from a mother, if not happiness? Arm in arm, they went into the dining room. It smelled like toasted bread. How beautifully the samovar was bubbling. It put Ali in mind of a factory where there were no strikes, no accidents, no sorrows. A factory that brought forth only fragrant steam and the joy of morning.

Ali loved the samovar, and he loved the *salep* kettle that stood outside the factory. He loved the sounds: the Halıcıoğlu Military Academy's trumpet and the factory whistle which went on for so long it could be heard the length and breadth of the Golden Horn. First they would awaken the flames of desire in him, and then they would put them out. That is to say, Ali was a bit of a poet. And while an electrician working in a big mill has as much space for poetry as the Golden Horn has for transatlantic liners, well – Mehmet, Hasan and I – we're all a bit like Ali. In each of our hearts, a lion sleeps.

Ali kissed his mother's hand. Then he licked his lips as if he'd tasted something sweet. His mother smiled. Every time he kissed her he would pass his tongue over his lips in exactly the same way. In the little garden outside, there was sweet basil growing in pots. Ali picked a few leaves and rubbed them in his palms, breathing in their fragrance as he stepped out into the street.

The morning was cool. Mist swirled over the Golden Horn. Ali's friends were waiting by the rowboats at the pier. All four were strong young men like him. Together they crossed over to Halıcıoğlu.

Ali has fire in him today, and joy, and fervor, and it will all go into his work. But he'll take care not to outshine his friends. For them he'll be honest, he'll take care not to show off. Otherwise he'd be putting on airs. His boss was once the only electrician in Istanbul. A German. He had taken a shine to Ali. He'd taught him all the tricks of the trade. If Ali had gained the respect of those who were just as able as he, it was because he was so agile, so fast, so playful and so young.

By evening he could go home happy, knowing that he was just the sort of friend his friends most needed, and just the sort of worker the bosses most trusted.

After embracing his mother, he was off to the coffeehouse across the street to see his friends. He played a hand of whist and then moved on to watch a game of backgammon. Then he headed home, to find his mother performing her evening prayers. And he knelt down beside her, like he always did. He turned a somersault over her prayer rug. He stuck out his tongue. When at last he had succeeded in making her laugh, she sat up to greet him.

"Ali, my darling, it's a sin!" she said. "My boy, it's a sin, so you mustn't!"

And Ali replied, "God will forgive us, Mother."

And then in a soft and innocent voice, he asked, "Doesn't God ever laugh?"

After supper, Ali curled up with a Nat Pinkerton novel and his mother went back to knitting him a sweater. And then they laid out their bedding, heavy with the scent of lavender, and drifted off to sleep.

Ali's mother woke him up at the morning call to prayer.

How beautifully the samovar was boiling in the room that smelled of toasted bread. It put Ali in mind of a factory where there were no strikes, no accidents, no sorrows. A factory that brought forth only fragrant steam and the happiness of morning.

·　·　·

Death came to Ali's mother with a guest's soft footsteps. It settled into the shadows, like a pious neighbor bending over to pray. In the morning she had made her son tea and by evening she had prepared two pots of food. Then, tugging at the edge of her heart, she felt an ache; hurrying up the stairs in her evening muslins, she could feel her worn body going soft, and moist, and limp.

One morning, when Ali was still asleep, she was standing over the samovar when all at once she fainted. She fell into a nearby chair. She fell, oh, she fell.

It was some time before Ali began to ask himself why his mother hadn't come to wake him up. Only then did he realize how late it was. The windowpanes had muffled the sharp, shrill blast of the factory whistle: it came to Ali's ears as if through a sponge. He jumped out of bed. At the door to the dining room, he stopped. He gazed at his dead mother, her hands flat on the table, as if asleep. And that was what he thought at first, that she must be asleep. Softly, he walked over to her. He took her by the shoulders. It was when he put his lips against her already cold cheeks that the first shiver went through him.

When we are confronted with death, we become great actors. Great actors, nothing more.

He threw his arms around her. He carried her to his bed. He pulled the quilt over her, tried to warm her body, which had already grown so cold. He tried to breathe life into her lifeless form. Later, giving up, he laid her out on the sofa in the corner. No matter how hard he tried, he couldn't cry that day. His eyes burned and burned, but not a single tear. He looked at himself in the mirror. At the moment of his greatest sadness, could he not be granted a face other than the one he saw staring back at him? It was the face of a man who had lost no more than a night of sleep.

All of sudden, Ali longed to grow thin, go gray, all of a sudden he longed to double over in agonizing pain as his face withered away. Then he looked again at the body. It didn't frighten him at all.

On the contrary: her face was as tender and kind as before. Her eyes were half open; with a firm hand he closed them. He ran out into the street. He told the old woman who lived next door. The neighbors came running into the house. He headed for the factory. By the time he boarded the caique that would take him across the Golden Horn, he seemed at peace with her death.

They'd slept side by side under the same quilt, shoulder to shoulder. In death they were just as close. In the same way death had come to his gentle mother, it left; with a guest's soft footsteps, it carried away her compassion and her warmth. She was just a little cold. We have nothing to fear, he thought. She was just a little cold. That was all.

For days, Ali paced the empty rooms of the house. He spent his evenings sitting in the darkness. He listened to the night. He thought about his mother. But he couldn't cry.

One morning they came face to face in the front room. How bright and peaceful this empty vessel looked, sitting there on the oilskin tablecloth, flashing copper sunlight. Picking it up by the handles, Ali moved it to a place where he couldn't see it. He collapsed into a chair. The tears came now, like silent rain. And the samovar never boiled in that house again.

From then on, Ali's life revolved around the *salep* kettle.

In Istanbul winters are harsher along the shores of the Golden Horn; the fog is denser. As they make their way to work in the early morning, over broken pavements and frozen clods of mud, the city's teachers and drovers and butchers and even the occasional student will often stop off for a few minutes outside the factory to lean against its great wall and sip *salep* sprinkled with cinnamon and ginger.

They cradle their glasses of *salep*, these rheumy fair-haired workers, these teachers and drovers and butchers and impoverished students. The steam passes through their woolen gloves, to warm their grateful hands. They lean against the great wall, dreaming of rebellion and steaming like mournful copper samovars, as they sip the *salep* that will later warm their dreams.

My Father's Second House

. . .

I had no idea why we went to that village house that day, to find a meal of duck, bulgur and semolina *helva* waiting for us in the kitchen. As I stand lonely and forlorn at this hotel window, watching the trams pass below, I still cannot say what it was that prompted our quiet evening visit to this village house, where we seemed to be expected.

In the neighboring village, they had already called the evening prayers. We'd watered our horses. Ever since leaving the city, my father had been in a foul mood. Everything seemed to bother him – the cloudy skies, the dusty roads and ditches. One word from me and we would have turned around, to race back through that quiet borough at a full gallop, the street dogs barking in our wake. Once we were home, with our horses safe in their stable, my father would have gone off to the town teahouse, and I to my room. To say nothing seemed to hold more promise. I kept the frown on my face, too. When my horse stumbled – only once or twice – I could see the wind ruffling my father's eyelashes. He didn't even blink. Had our eyes met like this on any other day, he would have mocked me with a fixed, false smile. His own horse never stumbled. When we reached that village house, there was a boy waiting for us. He was as delicate as lace. He took charge of our horses. Thinking that I was admiring the carnation he'd fastened to his cap, he offered it to me. Whereas I'd been looking at his eyes, which made me think of wet hay, and his face, which was the same color. Who knows, maybe he gave me the carnation because he knew he could never offer me the rest. Just then, my father turned his back. First I sniffed the carnation. Then, after I'd placed it between my cap and my ear, I saw my father looking back at me. He wasn't smiling. But he wasn't frowning, either. His face was without expression. He was oddly calm. I could have taken offense, it seems to me. I fixed my eyes on a male turkey. How big it looked in the half-light, with its featherless red neck. This creature must be very strong, I thought.

"Come on now, you fool," said my father under his breath.

The boy set off slowly with the horses, leaving us to enter the house.

We were met at the door by the sharp scent of hay and a faint hint of dung. Stepping toward the churn, we got a strong whiff of ripe yoghurt. We ascended a small staircase. And there, on a wooden balcony that looked like a pulpit or the sort of stage that a preacher might use for a public address on a national holiday, we found an old woman praying. My father paused on the fifth step, and I stopped two steps behind. We had taken our shoes off at the door; walking through the house in our woolen socks, we made no noise, I now realized. When this woman finished her prayers and stood up, she would suddenly find herself face-to-face with my father. When she saw his enormous shadow looming over her in the twilight, she would, I thought, scream loud enough to bring the whole village running. Nothing like that happened. Because we were standing on her right, she saw us as soon as she rose to finish her prayer. What I noticed first were the old woman's lips. As she stood there, blinking calmly, I looked at her eyes. Then I noticed the prominent bones in her temples. As she turned to the other side, my heart began to race, race like the wind. If only I had been close enough to smell her headscarf. It was made of that fine white muslin. The same as my grandmother's. The face she turned toward us now was soft and motherly. Gesturing at the door opposite with the same tenderness, she said:

"Ömer Ağa! Fatma's waiting for you inside."

And my father said, "Of course! And how are you? You're looking well, Granny."

The woman nodded; we went across to the room opposite. Here we found a young woman. She was singing a folk song to the night. When she saw us she rose with a smile.

In this room was the aroma of overripe fruit. In the light of the gas lamp, the red in the pattern of the Kocaeli kilim seemed to bubble, like some odd sort of jam.

With each new twist in this strange journey of ours, I became more curious, I was alert to every detail; but now my father turned to me and said:

"So, my son. You can go outside now. You can help Emin. And make sure the horses urinate before you put them in the stable."

The horses had urinated and were safe in their stables. They'd been given dry hay. Emin was still at the stable door. He was stripping a branch with a penknife. I went to sit next to him. He didn't look up. Thinking I might say something about the branch he was whittling, I noticed the anger in his hands. My eyes on the branch, I asked:

"What tree is that from?"

He didn't answer right away. He had cut his finger. He licked the wound for some time with his pink tongue that was as sharp and pointed as a cat's. Then he opened his cherry colored lips.

"It's from a dogwood," he said.

The conversation ended there. This fresh-faced child was as warm as a summer evening at the water's edge, and yet he seemed to regret our first moment of intimacy. A rough female voice called to us from the house. We went inside to eat roast duck, bulgur and semolina *helva* at a low wooden table. The towels were made from a thick cloth. There were wooden spoons. They had set out forks for my father and me. Not long ago, they informed us, there had been a strange and terrifying game of hide and seek with some wild boars in the cornfields, in the light of the moon. A pig had attacked a child the same age as Emin, splitting his stomach in two. The old woman told us the whole story, very slowly, naming the neighbors who owned the pasture where the incident occurred, naming the child, naming the hunters, one by one. My father wore an expression that told me he knew all these people. Emin kept looking at me. It was just us three at the table with the old woman. The young woman served us. Only when she put the pans on the table could I see the henna on her hands. We ate on the balcony where we'd found the old woman praying. After supper we went up to the top floor of the house, to a room with a stove. After he had lit this stove, Emin kneeled down on a black sheepskin rug. A moment later, he lay down on it and stretched himself out. The rug was just a little too short for him.

The old woman was half asleep on the cushions. I was lying next to her. My hand was in hers. Sleep passed through her hand into mine like a yellow sickness, closing my eyes. I could feel her submission, and her suffering, as I pried my hand free. I found a new place for myself, a bit further away from her, and closer to Emin.

All this while my father remained with the young woman on the divan. My father's cigarette would flare up now and again, amidst unearthly wreaths of smoke. They were talking about weddings, young girls, young men. The burning logs in the stove crumbled and lit up Emin's face. I fell asleep.

I awoke at daybreak. As we set out for the rich man's house that my father had first joined as a son-in-law, I could feel the steam of warm buffalo's milk on my face even as the morning mist swirled in to chill my cheeks, and I could still feel the lips of the old woman on my forehead, and the thick fingers of my brother Emin still joined with mine.

For a very long time, I was able to preserve that moment. Then the paper yellowed like a picture postcard, and the image faded.

The Silk Handkerchief

. . .

Moonlight shimmered across the silk factory's long façade. Here and there I could see people hurrying alongside it. But there was nowhere I wished to go. I was making my way out, very slowly, when I heard the watchman call out to me.

"Where are you off to?"

"I'm just going for a stroll," I said.

"Don't you want to see the acrobat?"

I hesitated, so he went on:

"Everyone's going. This is the first time anyone like him has ever come to Bursa."

"I'm not interested," I said.

He begged and groveled until I agreed to take his shift. For a while I just sat there. I smoked a cigarette. I sang an old folk song. But soon I was bored. I might as well stretch my legs, I thought. So I picked up the watchman's studded nightstick and went off to do the rounds.

I had just passed the girls' workshop when I heard a noise. Taking out my flashlight, I made a sweep of the room. And there, racing along the carpet of light, were two naked feet.

After I had caught the thief, I took him to the watchman's room, to get a good look at him in the lamp's yellow glow.

How tiny he was! When I squeezed his small hand in mine, I thought it might break. But his eyes, how they flashed.

I laughed so hard I let go of his hand.

Then he lunged at me with a pocketknife, slicing my pinkie. So I got a tight grip on the little devil and went through his pockets: some contraband tobacco and a few papers of the same sort, and a handkerchief that was almost clean. I dabbed some of his tobacco on the wound, tore a strip from the handkerchief and wrapped it around my finger. With the remaining tobacco we rolled two fat cigarettes and then sat down like two old friends and talked.

He was just fifteen. From which I was to understand that he was new to this business, he was just a boy. You know the story – someone had asked him for a silk handkerchief – a girl he loved, a girl he had his eye on, the girl next door. He couldn't just go out and buy one, he had no money. So after thinking the matter through, he'd decided on this.

"That's fine and good," I said. "But the workshops are on this side of the building. What was it that took you to the other side?"

He smiled. How could he have known which side the workshops were on?

We lit up two of my village cigarettes. By now we were good friends.

He was Bursa born and raised. He had never been to Istanbul – only once in his life had he even been as far as Mudanya. And, oh! To see the look on his face when he told me all this . . .

As a boy in Emir Sultan, I would often go sledding on moonlit nights, and this boy reminded me of the friends I had made there.

I could imagine his skin going as dark as theirs in the summer. As dark as the water in the Gökdere pools we could hear bubbling in the distance. As dark as the pits of summer fruit.

I looked at him more closely: His olive skin was as dark as a walnut fresh from its green shell. His teeth were as fine and white as the flesh inside. In summer, and right through to the end of walnut season, boys' hands smell only of peaches and plums in this place and their chests give off the aroma of hazel leaves as they roam the streets half-naked in their buttonless striped shirts.

Just then the watchman's clock struck twelve; the acrobat's show was nearly over.

"I should get going," the boy said.

I was just regretting having sent him on his way without a silk handkerchief when I heard a commotion right outside the door, and the watchman came in muttering under his breath, dragging the thief back in with him.

This time I held him by the ears, while the watchman whacked the soles of his feet with a willow switch. Good thing the boss wasn't there. I swear he would have called the police. "Thieving at this age," he'd have cried. "Well, the boy can smarten up in jail."

He looked scared by the time we were through with him – as if at any moment he might start crying. But he didn't shed a tear. His lips didn't tremble and his eyebrows hardly moved. There was only a faint fluttering of eyelashes.

When we let him go he took off like a swallow, vanishing as if he were soaring over a moonlit cornfield.

▪   ▪   ▪

In those days I slept in the storeroom on the floor above the workshop. How beautiful that room was. And never more so than on moonlit nights.

Just outside my window was a mulberry tree. Moonlight would come cascading down through its leaves, throwing flecks of light across the floor. Summer and winter I left the window open. The wind was never too rough or cold. I had worked on a ferryboat and I knew the different winds from their smells – the *lodos*, the *poyraz*, the *karayel*, and the *günbatısı*. So many winds swept over me as I lay on that blanket, each one bringing its own strange dreams.

I'm a light sleeper. It was just before daybreak when I heard a noise outside. Someone was in the tree, but I was too afraid to get up or cry out. A shadow appeared in the window.

It was the boy. Slowly he dropped down into the room and when he passed me I shut my eyes. First he went through my cupboard. Then, very slowly, he went through the stockpile. I didn't say a word. The truth is, even if he'd made off with everything, I could never have said a word in the face of such boldness. In the morning, the boss would beat the truth out of me. "Take that, you dog!" he'd say. He'd tell me a dead man could have done a better job, and then he'd fire me. I knew all this, but still I didn't say a word.

He slipped out through the window as quietly as he had come. Then I heard a snap. I rushed downstairs and found him lying in the moonlight, while the watchman and a few others looked on.

He was dying. His fist was clenched. When the watchman pried it open, a silk handkerchief shot up from his hand, like water from a spring.

Yes, that's right. That's what happens if a handkerchief is pure silk. Crumple it up as tight as you can. But open your hand, and it shoots right up, like water from a spring.

The Bohça

. . .

I remember the first day she came to our house. I was sitting under the mulberry tree, telling the neighborhood boys about my day in the water. My voice was shaking as I described my adventures on the coast. My passionate report had them rooted to the spot; none of these boys knew how to swim. Their eyes brimmed with questions. But I was feverishly certain that I could read their thoughts so I didn't give them a chance to say a thing.

I heard someone calling to me from the garden gate. And there she was. To hide my surprise, I kept on talking.

"Then I couldn't touch the bottom. I was swallowing water. But I wasn't at all scared. I was thinking of my next move."

"Young man, your mother wants to see you."

That's what she said.

"I'm coming," I said.

And I went right on telling my friends about how I nearly drowned while learning how to swim.

After they had left, I turned back to the garden gate. She was still standing there waiting, but her eyes were on a finch that was singing in the quince tree.

"Is that a nightingale?" she asked.

"No, girl, that's a finch."

She refused to believe me.

"I'm nobody's fool," she said. "That finch already flew away."

She had a rough way of speaking.

"Shut up, girl. Don't you have any manners? Don't joke like that."

She set her sad eyes on me and gave me a long, hard look.

I went into the kitchen. She followed me in. I tortured her with questions. Why was she here? "I used to be a wet nurse at Major Hidayet's," she said. In those words, more or less.

I can't tell you what a despicable little bourgeois brat I was in those days. I was set on making her suffer. There were bruises all over her olive-colored skin, and cuts. She had small, twisted hands with slender, purple-veined wrists that were covered in scratches.

There were times when I spat in her face, times when I slapped her. In spite of all the abuse I hurled at her, she never stopped being kind to me.

According to her birth certificate, she was one year older than me. The two of us were just scrawny kids full of mischief, and pretty much out of control.

One winter night she came to me in a dream. She was wearing a black dress, and her sun-bleached hair was draped over her chest, or, rather, it clung to her long and supple neck. Her breasts were no larger than turnips, and how pale her face, despite her olive skin, and such perfect feet. In those days there was a man I saw in my dreams whom I first identified as my grandfather, and later understood to be the old dervish saint, Nurbaba, or Father Christmas. In this dream, he took my hand and hers and joined them together.

"You two must stop fighting," he said.

With that, the old man lowered his bushy eyebrows until they touched the tips of his lashes. From then on we never quarreled again. It was the dream that did it – I want to make that clear. Yes, it was a dream. A dream that changed us.

We were holding hands under the mulberry tree. The finch was warbling in the quince. The sky above us sparkled with giant stars. A moon as large as a pebbly, reedy cove was hanging over the horizon and a lake. As we walked toward the moon, it merged with the shore.

That's as much as I can remember. Anticipation is clearer and crisper than the thing that lingers on our tongues. But as the dream began to fade, I did almost taste the strange fruit that once drove a man from paradise. Or so I recall.

The next morning I found the real sun hanging in the sky. I broke the ice in the garden fountain and I washed my face. But I still felt like I was dreaming.

Then I saw her in the courtyard, holding in her right hand a cloth we used for polishing shoes. Her face looked unwashed. Her almond eyes were swollen and there were spots on her neck that looked like flea bites.

I leaned over her as she polished my shoes and when my lips touched her hair I was gripped by a hunger I had never felt before. I pulled out a few strands of her hair, and as I walked to school I examined them, very closely. I might still have been dreaming. Half of each strand was jet-black, and the other half a warm yellow.

My conversations with her went something like this.

"Girl, you haven't polished my shoes."

"I swear I did, my young sir."

"I just said you didn't!"

She'd look at me standing there with those strands of hair in my hand – half black, and half yellow – and she would freeze. And collapse into silent tears. The more she cried, the angrier I would be.

"Girl, did you rip this?"

"I swear to God I didn't, my young sir."

"I say you did!"

I never gave her the chance to deny it twice.

"I was looking at the pictures, young sir!"

"Why?"

"Because I like them."

There was something I wanted to say to her one day, after she told me that. I can still remember the words. It went something like this: I like you, too, girl. I like you more than those pistachios I so adore but never share with you. But do I crack open the shell and eat those sweet green nuts, just because I love you?

"Girl!"

"What's wrong, young sir?"

"Nothing . . ."

"Young sir!"

"What's wrong, girl?"

"Nothing . . ."

We were standing together under the mulberry tree. We never did have a chance to talk to each other about nothing being wrong. But it seemed as if we both felt we had. She had her head in my lap, and her scent all around me. It was a summer afternoon when mother caught us there. I scrambled through the garden gate, ran down to the shore and stayed in the warm water till evening. Later I was back in the garden with the boys from the neighborhood. But this time, I had nothing to be excited about. Pretending to listen, I kept glancing over at the garden gate. But she never came out for me. Eventually the boys left. I walked back into the house. I went to look for her in the kitchen, but she wasn't there.

Everyone knew that she kept her *bocha* in a corner of the storage room. When something in the house was missing, it was the first place we would look. Without saying a word, we'd go through her *bocha* with its patchwork of red, white, yellow and navy blue squares.

I went into the storage room, heavy with the scent of oil. I looked for the *bocha*, but it was gone.

Wedding Night

. . .

Ahmet was sixteen, but his birth had yet to be registered. He had the flattest of noses and the narrowest of foreheads and jet black hair that shone with glints of midnight blue. He already had whiskers. Inside his navy serge suit, his body looked slender, athletic, and perfectly formed. When his father presented him to the registrar, the man did not hide his displeasure.

"Shame on you!" he said. "And why was it, I wonder, that you've taken so long to register this young man's birth? What sort of tricks did you pull during the census?"

During the census they'd hidden him in the hayloft. There had been rumors of another war. Ahmet was just twelve years old at the time, and their only son, but the army could still have taken him. That's what they'd reckoned. It had turned out differently, but what did it matter? Ahmet wasn't like Turkey's other children. Ahmet's father was Rüstem Ağa and even after the threat of war had passed, there had still been a need for precautions.

The registrar asked, "Is this boy twenty yet?"

It had been decided that sixteen-year-old Ahmet had been born in 1909. And that he was to marry a twenty-six-year-old woman born in 1911.

It was a dark autumn night, and the rain was pelting down. The sky was wandering the streets. A band of men holding lanterns was hurrying Ahmet across the village square, which was littered with the crushed husks of chestnuts. Pulling Ahmet to the back of the group, Black Abdi said his piece once again:

"Ahmet," he said, "I'm your best man. So now listen to me carefully." (Here he paused.) "When we've pushed you in there and closed the door on you, what you do next is kneel down on the rug and pray twice for God's blessing. Do you understand?"

The rain was really coming down now. The gutters were gushing, and the lanterns were far ahead of them. They had forgotten to look out for puddles. Their trousers were sopping wet.

The young men in the coffeehouse wiped the mist off the windows; seeing Ahmet pass by with his best man, they smiled. The old men, whose minds were on their taxes, rose to stand at the door, sending him on his way with strange jokes.

Ahmet was so startled that he fell into a pile of chestnuts and hurt himself. As Abdi lifted him up, he called out to the men who were racing away with their lanterns.

"Wait for us, will you?" Then, turning back to Ahmet, he said, "The rest you know. You're old enough, and big enough. Don't make me spell it out for you."

Ahmet said nothing. The chestnut thorns still stung. He was chewing on something, but were they questions, or were they chestnuts? It was hard to tell. His mind was fogged by the *rakı* they'd given him, and then they'd pulled him into this procession, and now their will was his command.

As they led him along, they showered this lean, solidly built and bright-eyed boy with taunts that seemed somehow serious.

Gülsüm's house was so very far away tonight. The rain was coming down even harder now. They were almost running. When at last they reached the house, the women inside threw open the door. The groom was covered head-to-toe in mud. The women brushed him off. His navy serge suit was now the same color as his hair. The wet, shiny down on his cheeks made this ugly child look almost handsome. He seemed to be wet from perspiration, not rain, and after he had wiped his face with a cloth, it looked red and polished like an apple.

His eyes were downcast; he was still picking thorns out of his hands. They brought him coffee and, paying no heed to Abdi's advice, he knocked it back. He hadn't trembled like this since his circumcision four years earlier. Then they brought him to his feet and, pounding with their fists on his back, they pushed him into a room, and then closed the door and left.

The room had a low ceiling and was lined with hanging bunches of grapes, apples, pears and quinces. There was almost no light, and the stench of fruit was so strong it made him dizzy. But it wasn't just the fruit. Hovering above it was the hint of fine muslin, a bride's dress, and a fine body underneath.

He went over to the open window and shut it, and for a moment he lingered, looking through the glass to watch the men and women coming out of each house to join the lantern procession. With his hands he wiped the fly droppings from the top of the dresser and adjusted the photograph of a soldier. He turned down the gas lamp. The woman was standing before him, utterly still. And now he caught sight of the prayer rug. Folding it up, he threw it into a corner. Pausing before the mirror, he looked at his red face. The woman was sitting by the window now. And there in the corner was the empty mattress, just like Black Abdi had predicted. "You are going to sit down next to her," Black Abdi had said, "and for an hour at least, you are going to talk to her." But what could he say to a girl he'd never met? His head was on fire, and his nerves were playing on the edges of his bones, one by one. Again, he examined himself in the mirror. For a long while he stared at the lantern wick, as if he were searching for something, and then, with one twist of his thick hands, he extinguished the flame. He could see the woman sitting by the window, staring out into the night and the rain.

Quietly Ahmet walked over to the bed and sat down next to her. He pressed his head into his trembling hands . . . He couldn't think. He could hear the rain pelting down, and the crowd outside growing louder, but everything else was spinning around inside him. The wheel was unraveling. He was falling down a well. The problem wasn't in his head, he thought. It was everywhere else. If only the dogs could stop barking, if only the rain would stop pelting down like this for just a moment, then he could think. Bright bolts of lightning cast the room in a blue light. Until now, he had thought himself locked in a room alone somehow, but now he saw the large frightened eyes of the woman sitting across from him. He began to wonder if that blue light came from inside this ghostly creature and her white muslin şalvar. Was it the chestnut thorns that were making his hands ache? Or was it that he'd eaten so much that evening? Was that why he felt so much pain and heaviness in his stomach? His sight was blurred, his mind fogged, his sweat cold. Seized by a malarial seizure, he curled himself up into a tiny ball.

Toward morning, he woke to find the woman curled up at the other end of the mattress, still dressed in her muslins, or almost.

Though the rain had lessened, it was still pouring down on the half-lit square. The dogs were still barking. The cattle were passing, their wet bells ringing in the mist. They were followed by gloomy shepherds, surrounded by goats and cowering under their sacks.

Gülsüm was awake now, too. She looked pale. She was trying to smile. The morning light from the window cast a mist over the hanging fruit. Ahmet was thirsty. He seized a bunch of grapes. With a second bunch of grapes in his hands, he approached the pale girl on the bed and popped two grapes into her mouth. How bright she looked in the half-lit room as, saying nothing, he pressed his thick, wet lips against her neck.

The sun rose, flickering in the mirror and their eyes. They opened the curtains.

The Barges

. . .

The crowds had gone. They were the last two men on the bridge. One was dressed like a laborer, and the other – who looked to be about the same age – like a sailor. They were sitting side by side, smoking in silence as they looked across the water in the direction of Üsküdar.

Üsküdar is best seen from a distance, and now, as it slept, its dark shores lit here and there by red lights, it looked so distant, and beautiful, as to be forever out of reach.

The sailor turned to his companion. "I have an aunt in Üsküdar," he said. "We could go over and visit her one day."

"Maybe. We'll see."

Sinking back into silence, they watched a motor launch pass beneath the bridge. The barges trailing behind it were carrying full loads, tied down with tarpaulin. They must have been carrying some sort of grain – wheat, or barley, or corn. They had that softness.

As the laborer watched the last barge slip under the bridge, he looked at the load that he had decided must be wheat, and for a moment was tempted to jump into that softness. He tried to hold the words back. But couldn't.

"I wish I'd jumped right in," he said.

"Just like in the movies, eh?"

The laborer didn't answer. He didn't answer, but he smiled.

It was a winter night in the middle of Ramadan. Turning together to look at the old city, they looked at the lights strung up between the minarets.

"I love those lights," the sailor said.

And the laborer said, "So do I."

On weekends one of these men would take himself off to Galata. The other to Şehzedebaşı . . . On very rare occasions, they would come together to the bridge to watch the night. They whiled away the night watching the lights of Üsküdar and the great ships of Galata, the smaller vessels tied to the piers, and the motor launches pulling barges that were sometimes empty, sometimes full. They knew from these evenings that they could count on one another; just by exchanging four or five sentences, they knew they were good friends.

Each time the laborer came here and saw a barge loaded down with wheat, he had to fight the urge to climb over the railings and drop himself into it. Sometimes he would say this to his friend, and his friend would say:

"Just like in the movies, eh?"

Then they would go home, or, if they had this conversation early enough, they would suddenly remember a movie house in Yüksekkaldırım, and so they'd go there and sit together in the front row.

No matter what film was showing, it left them happy and smiling. They didn't say a word on the way home. And that night one of them would dream of kissing his Galata friend like the tough guy in the film. Meanwhile, the other dreamed of taking his friend to the darkest street of Şehzedebaşı and burying his nose in the palms of his hands and kissing them. These dreams would rob them both of sleep and make wrecks of them.

"Did you sleep well?" one would ask.

And the other would say, "I sure did."

If one of them smiled, the other would fall asleep right away. If he didn't, he was already asleep.

It was a white, moonlit night. Light puffs of smoke were rising from the ferries docked along the pier. They made a man yearn to set out on a long journey. Now and then a ferry would approach the pier and behind it a second ferry, lit by a second light, to send a flurry of passengers up and down the gangplank.

Suddenly, the laborer said:

"Why don't we go with them?"

The other said:

"Let's go, then."

They slept in the same room. One was from Sivas. The other from Izmir. One worked at the pier, tying up the ferries as they docked. The other worked in a mill. The room they shared cost them four lira a month but they never once spent an evening in. They hardly ever saw each other. One finished work at nine. The other would come back at twelve and go straight to sleep. The room was pitch black. Hardly any daylight came in through the grilled window that looked out onto a grimy, musty courtyard. One man's bed was on the right-hand side of the room, and the other man's bed was on the left. Because he had no quilt, the laborer slept in his clothes. The other slept in his shirt and shorts.

One had to be back on his ship by six in the morning. The other started work after noon. If ever they both woke up at six, the sailor, whose boss was a Greek, would say:

"And a fine *kalimera* morning to you, my son."

Not knowing that *kalimera* was Greek for good morning, and thinking his boss had said *karamela*, the laborer would respond with his own bit of nonsense: "One caramel for me, and one caramel for you!" And together they would laugh.

One day they fired the sailor. A falling out with a harbor official. This was all he told his friend:

"He called me a son of a donkey, and I smashed his jaw."

His friend said:

"I wish you hadn't done that."

These words so upset the man that he went for three days without eating, and without asking his friend for help. The other thought he must be living on his savings, so he didn't ask him how he was. Then the sailor found work in the Paşabahçe glass factory. He was going to board there, too, and so he bid his friend farewell. They embraced each other. That last evening, they went out again to the bridge.

"We never made it over to Üsküdar to see my aunt," the sailor said.

"No, we didn't, did we?" said the man from Sivas. "But maybe we'll still get there one day, my dear friend!"

How beautiful the moon looked in the sky above. It could tear a man up just to think about how strange it must be, up there on the moon. If only we were there, just the two of us, they thought, if only it was just the two of us, safe inside that moon . . . But neither man spoke. Neither man could find the words. Just then, they heard a motor launch puttering across the smooth waters. And behind it, barges. Again, carrying wheat. The laborer gazed down at the wheat-laden barges passing just beneath them. But this time he had no desire to jump in.

Nightwork

. . .

Ömer lunged at the woman with a curse that was swallowed up by the northwest wind, the same wind that had earlier ripped the bandana from his head. But it still made the youngest boy in the tavern jump. Next to him was a man of about forty-five, who said:

"Sit down, my child."

The youth looked up fearfully. This man did not want to kidnap him: he wanted his soul.

The drinking had begun well before nightfall. The trams had long since put on their lights, but as always Ömer still kept the lights turned off in the tavern. It was easier to talk and drink in this half darkness.

Eventually, the lights came on, timidly and one by one, but almost of their own accord, without the flick of a single switch. With each five-watt bulb taking five or ten minutes to light up, it was an hour before they were flickering in the darkness, casting light on Ömer's foul temper.

Once the lights were on, the tavern took on its usual appearance. It was, Ömer thought, noisier than hell. There were gangsters, laborers, fisher-men, and Greeks and Armenians of uncertain trades; they talked about everything, though their lips were sealed. In this tavern even the innocent could hear thieves and pickpockets plotting their business without fear or loathing. In the tavern's mirrors, they could look into the eyes of those turned away from the crowd, who were curled up, and unable to walk, and in those eyes you could see memories of an incident, an assault, a murder.

The woman whom Ömer had just cursed was rubbing her crimson cheek.

"Ömer Ağa, what came over you just now? I never meant to offend you. You took it the wrong way."

"I know exactly what you meant. And I can handle my own business."

Now Karabet the fiddler stepped inside. This was a man the gangsters respected. In their eyes he was an artist. Large or small, they all looked up to him. In his face, his clothes, and his manner, there were still the traces of the many years he'd spent in prison as a young man, and it was manifest in the music he played for them.

"Stand a little to the side, at least," Ömer told him.

Karabet might have seen this as an insult. Had Ömer pressed one of the gangsters like this, they would've been all over him. The fiddler moved to the side but made it clear that he was ready to draw his blade. Ömer pointed at the singer with the reddened cheek.

"Don't poke your finger into men's business ever again, do you hear?"

It was a woman sitting just behind who answered on the singer's behalf: she had bright eyes, crooked teeth, and bleached blond hair; she was old and Greek, but still as sociable as a cat.

"Don't worry, Ömer," she said, pressing one hand to her cheek, as if in pain, "Don't you worry one little bit. Zehra here is never ever going to poke her finger into men's business again."

She played it for laughs, and she did such a good job of it that even the solemn-faced Karabet cracked a smile. As she sank into her chair, Zehra muttered, "Whore!" between her teeth. Even Ömer laughed as he came down the steps from the musicians' stage. The tavern, which had fallen silent, now filled with laughter, as if on cue. The stink of rancid olive oil and anise wafted back into the room and soon it was as if nothing had happened. The gangsters drifted back to their intimate conversations, heroic tales, and love stories, pouring out their hearts. Except for two strangers gazing absently out the far window. One of them called over the waiter to ask, "What happened?"

As if sharing a secret, the waiter bent over and whispered into the man's ear. This man then whispered the news to his friend, as lightly as if he were cooling their *meze* with his breath.

"That woman . . . apparently she pointed at that young man over there, and said that Ömer must have turned him the other way."

The two men looked cautiously at Ömer's table. He was staring into his *meze*, lost in thought, while the hard-faced forty-five-year-old man next to him offered him consoling words, with calming gestures. Next to this man was a youth who looked to be about twenty. His cheeks were pink and plump, his skin white. When he smiled he looked ugly, there was a gold tooth that every now and then shimmered in the back of his mouth. His eyes were dull and without luster. His hair was soft. His shoulders were narrow, his manner rough, but for all his swaggering, there was something of a woman in him.

By the time Ömer left the tavern with the forty-five-year-old man, it was very late. They wandered drunkenly through the damp November streets, hearing no one.

Turning to his companion, Ömer said, "Get rid of this one. He's a worthless piece of shit. A coward."

The forty-five-year-old man turned to the youth who was three paces behind them, shoulders hunched.

"Go home, my boy, and get some sleep."

The boy vanished with the wind, saying nothing. The men continued in

silence until they reached the shore. Here there were boatmen, still waiting for customers despite the late hour, but when they saw these two they
made no offers. After jumping across several rowboats, the men reached
out for a guard rail. They pulled up a cover, and warm air hit their faces. In
the pitch dark below, they could hear snoring; as they made their way in,
the embers of cigarettes lit up a few faces. They stopped short in front of
one of them, as if they were surprised to see him, and knelt down before
him. This man was tall, tall as a corpse. His face was white and in the light
of his glowing cigarette it was like a painting made of broken glass. He
sucked in on his cigarette and then stubbed it out.

"Idris. Hey, Idris!"

Yawning on his bed, the man looked around. His voice was soft and
calm.

"Who are you? Why are you here?"

"Get up, Idris. It's me . . . Ömer."

"Who's that next to you?"

"Who do you think? It's Mavro."

"Oh, Mavro, is it? What's up?"

"What do you think? We have work to do."

"What work?"

"Nightwork, you fool!"

The tall man searched for his shoes. The damp of the night came through
the open hole that they now slowly climbed through. After jumping again
from rowboat to rowboat, they reached the muddy shore. Here Ömer
asked for the time.

Someone said, "It's half past eleven."

They began to walk. Everything was shut, and all they could hear were
the whistles of the night watchmen and the indistinct rustlings of night,
and ghostly footsteps.

They arrived at an all-night coffeehouse. From the outside it looked as if it were lit by a gas lamp, but there was just the one twenty-five watt light bulb, and the people inside could barely see each other. But once inside, the overwhelming stench of misery needed no illumination.

"Ali! Hello!"

In a Persian accent, someone said, "Ömer Ağa! How good to see you!"

"Fine, then. Three teas for us, if it's fresh. Where is the *simit* seller?"

"He'll be back any minute. My tea is freshly brewed."

Two tiny naked creatures were asleep on the sofa. Even in the darkness, you could see that they weren't covered, and though the coffeehouse was warm, they were shivering. Ömer stepped over to these creatures; in the darkness he could only see their noses, which were as small as watermelon seeds.

"So what are these, Ali?"

Ali went to Ömer's side, his face stricken.

"Street children, the poor things. We had to take them in. What else could we do?"

Ömer turned around to look Ali straight in the eye. Then with his giant hands he tugged the rug off the wall.

"So that you don't pity them free of charge," he said. "Throw this rag over them. Can't you see they're going to freeze?"

Once covered with the rug, the little boys burrowed into it without waking. Turning around to hug each other, they sank into the deep sleep of childhood.

In front of the stove was an opium addict who made his living selling fish off the end of the bridge. He was silent, lost in his dreams. Fish, huge fish, each one as big as a monster, seaweed that made their lures sparkle beneath the green sea, a caique laden with harbor prawns, mermaids, whelks as big as giants . . .

Next to him was a dark-eyed child of fourteen or fifteen. His curly hair was blacker than black. He wasn't sleeping, he was staring at the embers of his cigarette. Ömer went over to sit next to him. The others sank into chairs and were soon half asleep.

Then there was a little incident, so small that it disturbed neither the silence in the coffeehouse nor the sleeping opium addict. Springing to his feet, in his hand the switchblade he'd taken from the palms of another, Ömer cried, in a voice as calm as it was assured:

"We were just joking, Karayel! We were just joking!"

The child sitting next to him took in a breath, as deep as the sea. He spoke like the wind.

"I can't take jokes like that, Brother Ömer. For jokes like that, I've thrown seven knives. And seven knives have come back."

In his strange Black Sea accent, the swarthy boy kept talking about his lowly, coarse, deceitful deed. Ömer looked at him with a surprised smile.

"It was a joke. A joke! Karayel. Don't I know you? Ali, go make us another four teas. And go find the *simit* seller and bring him back."

Ömer had a hard time persuading the boy that it was all a joke. But now they were four people, sitting together in a huddle. Four people speaking in whispers too low for anyone else to hear. Until Mavro raised his voice to say to the one next to him:

"So there you have it. Just the boy we were looking for. He'll know what he's doing, too. All he has to do is give us one quick whistle."

Then there was more whispering, again loud enough to hear. When Ali came back from looking for the *simit* seller, he found them on their feet. Biting into their warm *simits* as they stepped into the street, they vanished into the night.

Who Cares?

. . .

Seen from below, the house up on the hill seemed perfect. It was the sort of house that a grocer or a businessman or a rake might dream about during his youth, or a retired teacher or a novelist, churning out great works – the sort of house where an exiled politician might wish, in vain, to end his days.

It opened onto a road that almost looked as if it had been created by the fallen rocks themselves. On a Sunday you might see a courting couple or two, but on other days, it seemed to recede into itself, affecting that odd anonymity that is not unique to roads. There are a few islanders who like to come this way, but even they prefer to walk the road after dark, to watch the stars – or so it seems to me.

On one side of the road is the least visited part of the island: a place where the pine trees grow into each other. There's no room even for a path. That's why you find no naughty lipstick-soiled handkerchiefs under the pine trees, or newsprint, or sardine cans. On the other side of the road is what seems from a distance to be a beautiful house: on closer inspection it turns out to be two ugly houses. Both sit on the side of the road, hemmed in on all other sides by the forest.

From a distance you might think that those dwelling inside these houses had come to fulfill dreams of living happily ever after, smelling the pines and the north wind, or that they had come to sell chickpeas or lull themselves to sleep under a pine tree, dreaming of a nation free of pines and all else, but no one beyond chickpea sellers seemed to know. That's how quietly they lived in these houses. In winter, when the village barber saw a sallow-faced man in his middle years running toward the ferry just as it arrived, he would turn to his customer and say, "That's the old man who lives in the house on the hill." What gossip they had all came from this. The old man would return with his arms full of small parcels and then he wouldn't come down for weeks. And the island's year-round inhabitants below would engage in their usual gossip and backbiting, until the fishermen came from the Black Sea and they stopped; instead they would try to rent out their rooms to them, on the sly. Unless it was rented on the sly, it could not be rented in the summer to visitors coming to the island to relax and swim in the sea. Because fishermen are bachelors. Bachelors, and also fishermen . . . True or not, fishermen's shirts were said to be infested with lice.

It was on one of those days when the island's year-round inhabitants were struggling not to disclose to each other the secrets on the tips of all their tongues – who had rented houses to the fishermen, and who was to say nothing on this subject before the summer visitors arrived – when they realized that no one had seen the sallow-faced old man in town for weeks and weeks.

It was one of those beautiful clear winter days. The fishermen had gone off to the city. The streets were empty, except for a woman whose face seemed quite young, though her blond hair was tinged with white. The coffeehouse owner was having a shave, between customers, and when he saw her he said:

"So who's this woman?"

The barber examined her closely, his narrow eyes flashing like lightning. As if to say, good God, who is she? As if to say, don't I know her?

"I can't place her," he said instead.

The woman looked first toward the coffeehouse. Two local fishermen, both Greeks, were playing backgammon in the corner. The coffeehouse owner inside was getting a shave. After glancing through the window, the woman raced for the pier. One of the fishermen noticed her.

"That's the wife of the man who lives on the hill."

And the others said, "You don't say!"

The woman went over to the harbormaster. She told him that her husband had died the day before, and that her children were going hungry. She asked for some help with his funeral and burial. The harbormaster told himself that this was the first time anyone had come to him with such a request. This was not someone asking him to arrange a free pass, nor was it a bill of goods upon which he could slap a fine of five or ten lira.

"What can I do about something like that?" he said. "My job is to be here for the ferries."

"Aren't you a Muslim?"

"Of course we are Muslims, Madam. Praise be to God! But we are also harbormasters. I cannot leave my post. It is my duty to stay here. Please go and talk to the main porter."

The main porter lived in a handsome two-story house in the middle of the village. As she approached the house, the woman looked as if she had something to say to the flames rising from the stove. At one moment it even looked as if she were standing in a room lit by a stove, plucking yellow – amber yellow – tobacco from a bowl, wire by wire, and relating the village gossip.

She knocked on the door.

Sitting before the potbellied stove with two children, a boy and a girl, at either side, was a swarthy man reading an old and yellowing newspaper. He was wearing glasses. Poking out from underneath his nightshirt were hairy, Herculean calves. One was resting on the other; one of his slippers had fallen to the floor. The exposed foot was extraordinarily ugly; it looked up at the woman, bruised and bulbous, like a newborn child.

"So Madam. Tell me why you're here."

The woman repeated what she'd said to the harbormaster. "Last night, my husband . . ."

"Madam," said the porter. "Do you have any money? It'll be hard, convincing any of my porters to go out there in the dead of winter. The rascals just won't budge! They're all going hungry. They've long since spent their summer earnings. They get no share of the fish, they could die of hunger. I could do something for you. I could, but not for nothing."

"I have nothing left to sell. I told you. I don't even have food for my children."

"You must be able to find some money somewhere."

"If I had the money to get to Istanbul, then perhaps . . ."

"Well, then. Here's ten, eleven *kuruş*."

The woman thanked him and took her leave. She ran to the bakery. With a loaf in her arms, she headed up the steep hill. A young girl ran up to her and buried her head in the woman's skirt. Bread that wouldn't fill her for more than ten minutes.

The woman went back down to the village. She'd remembered the district doctor. The district doctor was in the midst of his winter chemistry experiments. He'd dissolve his nitrates, turn litmus papers from blue to red, and from red to blue, produce chlorine, do an analysis of his water, check his blood pressure, sniff ozone.

When they told him a woman had come to see him, he was conducting a urine analysis. He had added some substances to the urine to find out if there was any sugar.

Eventually gases emerged from the liquid as it turned blue. Then suddenly the urine turned brick red.

"Oh, no!" said the doctor to himself. "We're in trouble! Now why did I drink that water? No sleeping now! My God grant us our just desserts!"

Poking her head through the door, his wife said, "There's a woman here to see you, sir."

"I'm coming," he said.

"I'll make it clear to this woman that she shouldn't be disturbing me like this," he mumbled to himself, "I'll show her . . ."

"So tell me. What seems to be the problem, Madam?"

The woman told him.

"He can't be moved until I see him."

"But he's not ill. The man's dead."

"We shall see if he's dead or not. How else could I know?"

"At the very least, ask them to move him."

"I can't go all the way out there. I'm ill, too, Madam. I'm diabetic. I'm old, the trek up there would do me in. Find me a donkey, and then I could come out. Without a donkey, I'm not budging."

"All right," said the woman as she left. "I'll try to find a donkey."

As she stepped outside, the woman saw with amazement that the morning's summery spell had ended most abruptly. A stinging wind had blown in. The clouds were rolling toward their house in the woods, one after the other, like a great funeral procession. She ran home. Rolling the body in a sheet, she carried it outside. It had begun to snow. In the space of a minute, her nightdress had turned white. She half carried, half dragged him as far as the top of the hill. Passing over it, she went down the other side until the ground was flat again. She was sheltered from the wind there. Here again, it was almost like summer.

It was quiet in this valley, and almost warm. Here and there, a snowflake swirled through the warm air. Only the south wind came as far as this cliff top. The north wind reached only as far as the tops of the evergreens.

A bit further along, there were more cliffs. And there, at the edge, the woman stood quivering – perhaps she was praying, or perhaps she was just cold. At first she could hear nothing. Then she did. But it was only pebbles, rolling down to the sea.

It snowed for three days. For three days, the wind howled. In three days, only three ferries stopped at the island. The head porter sat in front of his stove reading two-year-old newspapers, popping corn. The doctor ate at least a bit of pilaf every day, on the pretext of testing his urine. He just about forgot that a woman had come to see him.

The harbormaster was a thin, dry, nervous man. Now and again, something flamed up inside him. One moment he would remember this woman who had come to him, asking him to help her bury her husband, and the next moment he would forget.

But whenever the memory hit him, it was as if he were seeing his own body, dead for days, and still unclaimed.

It was another unseasonably warm day. The barber stopped shaving his customer and, pointing out the window with the tip of his razor, said, "There's the woman from the house on the hill again. Where's she off to this time?"

The sallow-faced woman was heading to the pier. Then she stopped. Instead, she began to walk along the shore. An old man was doing the same. He looked like one of those men who used the good weather as an excuse to come out to the islands for a stroll.

The woman walked straight over to the man. She seemed to want to tell him something. Then she gave up on the idea, smiling to herself as if something amusing had just occurred to her, and set off for the ferry that was just coming around the edge of the next island.

She was the only woman on the ferry, and the only one without a ticket. But the number of passengers disembarking at Kadıköy was the same as the number of tickets. Not a single ticket more, not a single less.

On Spoon Island

. . .

Mücahit was at the head of the rowboat, holding two little oars. I was bent over at the very bottom because rowboats always made my head spin. I couldn't see the water. All I could see was the bright sky above me shifting like running water. Odisya was singing something in Greek. Yakup was naked from the waist up and seemed to be listening. Sometimes moonlight flashed across his blue eyes. A boy whose name I didn't know was sitting beside me. He had an unusually small face and his body was small. Every part of him was small: his hands, his ears and his eyes. We called him "Sultan Hamit's dwarf."

We were crossing over to Spoon Island. Robinson's ghost was whirling inside us: Our ship had sunk and we were on a raft, we were bound for a deserted island, where we'd build a hut . . .

Reluctant to share our secret Robinsons, we all fell silent; the better to keep the dream alive. Seven of us on the boat, seven Robinsons in disguise. A single word would remind us that we lived on Burgazada, and that just an arm's length away there was Spoon Island, which looked like an overturned spoon in the moonlight – it belonged to a man; that because he had no heirs the island would fall into the hands of the state when he died; that though the island was deserted then, it would eventually end up in the hands of half a dozen people; that they would build houses and maybe even clear the land for beaches. This enormous imaginary transatlantic liner we had built from huts and rafts and dreams and savagery would come crashing into an iceberg. Never again would we set out for Spoon Island by moonlight in search of adventure. Instead we teased Yakup and he stopped pulling off his shirt and dressing up like a savage, and he stopped trying so hard to shape his dreams to fit with ours.

When I raised my head, I saw that we were gliding into a bay with white rocks glimmering at the bottom of the sea. And there before us was a white building. Were our eyes fooling us? A building on a deserted island? Still no one said a word. Even Odisya's Greek song died away. The little dwarf had rolled himself into a ball. The ones at the oars were angels soaked in sweat. Yakup wore the pride of an emperor. The children at the oars looked like slaves and Mücahit a cruel slave trader with a whip. The moment we stepped onto the sand, Yakup called us together:

"This building is an ancient Portuguese fort," he said. "Portuguese pirates were the first to discover the island. They came and left the youngest one of their party behind. The fierce young pirate had disobeyed his king. Walk quietly. He might still be alive. Some say there's a savage tribe on the island. We must be careful."

Odisya and Yakup played the savage and the Portuguese pirate. They suddenly disappeared. Jackal went after them, barking. I was left alone with Sultan Hamit's dwarf. The three other boys had set off for the old white building.

Spoon Island is full of cisterns. It's very dangerous to run across the island, especially at night. We didn't want to tumble down into the deep, dark water of a cistern hidden among the long weeds that swayed on the hilltops. So we watched where we stepped. The dwarf and I reached the top of the island. For a moment we stopped to look. In the distance, we could see that our three boys had lit candles in the windows of the white house. Further on, we could see the young Portuguese pirate's mansion, built when the island was a farm with pig stables and wire fences, and later abandoned. It was far too dangerous to go inside. A gardener's shed stood ten or fifteen meters in front of the stables. We could see it from where we stood. A light appeared in the window and we slowly made our way. We knocked on the door. Odisya opened it; he was alone with his dog. He had wrapped a garland of weeds around his head. He was wearing a baggy, striped shirt, and with his tanned chest, his bare feet, his blue eyes, his delicate and slender face, he was more of a pirate than Yakup would ever be. He was as beautiful and as savage as a pirate's child. I was overcome by the desire to be one of his bandits. His most brilliant bandit. He was our king. Beyond the door I could see across to a beach on Heybeli that reminded me of a lovely little public square, and whose lights were slowly fading like the lights on a massive ferryboat.

Odisya began singing again. Yakup and the other children would listen to him till the end, then the little ones would find us and make us slaves; then we would lay siege at the Portuguese Manor and force surrender. Odisya would sing again, and Yakup would tell a story. Then we would go home. We would argue on the way back. Yakup would refuse to speak to the ones who had spoiled the game; Odisya wouldn't sing and little Dwarf wouldn't indulge us with his funny games.

We three – Odisya, Yakup and I – were the only real islanders. The others lacked the patience for friendship and adventure in particular. Yakup's parents would hear about it, and they would try to stop us from setting out to the island. That's why our numbers could suddenly drop to three. But still we'd jump in the boat and cross over. Sometimes we'd stay until morning.

Jackal waited at the white building's open door while we slept inside, spinning our dreams from torn fishnets, corks and hooks. None of us ever told the whole truth. I only understood Greek. Odisya spoke good Turkish, and Yakup knew the odd broken, sweet phrase in Greek.

Odisya was the son of a gardener. He was the best swimmer among us, and he could fish, sing, row, and he had the best smile. He was a strange one. His mood could go sour without warning. It upset him enormously not to be taken seriously. The tiniest slight could turn his mood sour. The most innocent little word could cause him grave offense. Most of all he liked to fight. His face would turn yellow with confusion. He'd begin to stutter. Monsters didn't scare him, and neither did people; other children might tremble at the thought of savages and Portuguese pirates, but not he . . . He was different with children and eccentrics: he treated them with respect. It angered me to see how the little ones made fun of him. They undid him: the courage he carried in his wild face and blond hair and muscular arms suddenly splintered. I think Yakup liked Odisya because he found him useful. He might need Odisya to take care of something for him, something low and dirty that he couldn't do himself. He would get Odisya to do it by taunting him, saying he wasn't man enough for the job.

One day we couldn't find Jackal anywhere on the island so we crossed over to Spoon Island. We spent the night there.

Yakup said to Odisya:

"Just to be sure, you stand guard there by the door until the sun comes up. You can sleep during the day, and we'll wait for you. Maybe the savages will attack!"

Odisya wasn't a fool. But he was happy to play the part if it meant being a hero or doing a good deed for someone else.

Half asleep, I looked over and saw that Odisya was still awake. But before the sun came up, I lay down next to him and took his hand. Abruptly he rested his warm head on my chest and said:

"If my dad wasn't some grunt of a gardener I'd be a real man like you guys, I'd go to school, and if I knew how to read I'd keep reading and never sleep."

I lifted his head to the left. There were tears in his eyes. He let go of my hand. He got up and walked over to the pomegranate tree.

"I can't sleep, Odisya," I said. "Why don't you get some sleep now?" He lay down under the pomegranate tree. I lit what was probably the second or third cigarette I had smoked in my life. And he had already fallen asleep.

The moon was back up in the sky. It was the first time I had ever watched someone sleep. But he wasn't just anyone – he was an angel, a little man, pure and simple. I can still picture him now . . . dreaming his way through a world of peace and goodness and beauty. His waking world – that could make you tremble. But though I am awake, I swear I am sleeping his sleep. There I am with his heroes and his loved ones and the giant weeds and the fish and the sea; here now is a boat, and there, in front of the gardener's shed, is a large-breasted woman, and a winegrower with his fat moustache and his breath reeking of tobacco and wine, and inside the shed is a pile of clean but broken furniture; and here was his wiry, olive-skinned sister with her windblown skirt fluttering over her thin long legs, and I feel close to her, and the pine trees and arbutus berries and all else I have seen. Desire bubbles up in me like water from a spring. I am leaning over. I am kissing my friend on the cheek, his eyes are shut and his lips open. For the first and last time, I am kissing someone with a desire that is as pure as it is secret. Then I am running up to the Portuguese pirate's house to sleep. But I am a child, and I feel the Portuguese pirate might really be there and so I am vigilant. Silent as a mouse, I approach the house. The bottom of the window is at eye level and I look in. Moonlight is cascading across the room through another window; a young woman is sitting on one side of the room and a young man has his head in her lap, and she's caressing his hair; he keeps trying to kiss her free hand. I watch for a moment, hardly believing my eyes. Then I head down the hill, skipping over the rocks, and I race to the shed where Yakup is sleeping. I wake him and say, "Up there . . . there's . . . " Yakup asks me about Odisya:

"The fool. What's he waiting for?"

"Don't torture the poor kid. He's a good boy."

"I know better than anyone else that he's a good boy. I'm doing it on purpose, I only treat him like this because I love him. He'd do anything for the experience. What's he doing?"

"I just woke up. I told him to get some sleep. He's sleeping now."

"He never went to sleep? What a fool!"

We go over to see Odisya. Yakup looks him over carefully. As carefully as if he were dreaming his beautiful dreams. He leans over and caresses Odisya's hair:

"Let him sleep then. Let's go and have a look."

In the shed on the hill, it's the same as before. The boy in the girl's lap is trying to kiss her hands. When he turns his head in our direction, we take a step back. Her head is still, bowed. She is looking down at the boy. When the young boy turns again we duck. A shadow seems to fall over Yakup's face, which until then was strange, smiling and swirling with desire.

"He's my age."

"Who?'

"The guy in her lap."

For a moment we stand there upright, our eyes fastened on the scene. Then we step back. Yakup speaks, lost in thought:

"He's just my age, man!"

I don't say a word.

Winter drove our dreams into the rain, the snow, the cold, and the dark; some of us were at school, some of us were apprentices at corner shops, some of us were trudging through fog-covered fields of spinach, some of us were like Yakup, at the head of a boat, the sail billowing against a *lodos* or a *poyraz* . . .

From winter to summer a person can change beyond recognition. Most people grow fatter, and paler; some take on alarming new shapes . . . It seems to me that children never change over the summer, only over the winter do they grow.

We almost never saw each other that winter. By spring Odisya had grown tall, and in his face I could see the sinuous traces of a trickster. He was still singing but he had lost that crystal clear voice. That voice that had once drawn me into a warmer, sunnier world now sounded like the voice of a village trickster, a throaty, snaky, swaggering voice that sang of wine and greed and lies and gossip and lust and sleepless nights. It was as if he had thrown off the warm and open face that had once held me captive and discarded it like an old shirt; the face I saw now was the one I feared. It was the face of his uncle Manoli, the face he wore that week he spent trying to sell a lobster. Once I remember marvelling at how one face could evoke a world of sun and warmth, while another face, even a face that bore a close resemblance, could only convey the cold of the world we lived in. Back then I think I drew a line between a person's face and his character. That is not to say I thought beauty and good character went hand in hand. A wicked soul performs its sorcery best when it can hide behind a beautiful face. What I am trying to say is this: the facial gestures, even color and subtle movements that bespeak morality, are only there when the face is as true as the soul shining through it. The traits are then quite charming. And if the soul remains true, your friend will be pure, and easy to love, and almost too sweet to be true. But how wonderfully beautiful was the look on Odisya's face when he was exploring the real world back then: his nose crumpled up at a new scent and his mouth hung half open as he listened, trying to make sense of his discoveries. But today the same movements of his face are easily likened to his uncle Manoli and his impertinence, his jealousy and his deceit.

The fourth time I saw him, my regret knew no bounds. Oh, why did I do that? I couldn't stop asking myself. Why ever had I kissed that boy? How could I have ever loved that face?

Yakup had changed, too. Completely. Now he had as thick a neck as that boy we'd seen with that girl in the stable on Spoon Island. Somehow the barber had changed the color of his dark hair. He still hadn't shaved his moustache. And the barber had trimmed it into the oddest-looking thing. Despite all the unfortunate changes in his outward appearance, you could still see the old Yakup. When I looked into his face, I could still see traces of the adventures we'd shared. No, they were more than just traces. But not a word about Spoon Island. Now all he wanted to talk about were his adventures with a young girl:

"Eftehia's legs were as desperate to burn as yellow church candles, her crisp white teeth were as white as fresh walnuts, and her hands asked to be kissed."

Yakup met Eftehia in the autumn, when those arbutus berries I told you about were at their ripest. The bushes with blooming red flowers. Together they collected berries. Eftehia always took the ripest, plumpest berries. And then she was drunk, like all the other island women who said the berries made you drunk. She brought a ripe berry to her lips, took a bite and said to Yakup, "Now you eat the other half." Then they lay down as the scent of honey wafted over them from the bushes' red flowers.

Eftehia's face was the face of an ordinary Greek girl. Full of fire, nothing more. She wasn't very beautiful, and she wasn't ugly either. But when she was in the sea in her dark blue bathing suit, the sight of her little breasts, and the rounded, cruel curves of her lustrous, powerful legs could make a boy double over and drive his hands into the earth, and tear up the grass with his teeth . . . how beautifully she swam. When the island's summer houses filled up with dashing young men who dressed in sparkling whites, Eftehia quietly moved on from Yakup, who dressed in thick grays and had holes in his trousers. Odisya, meanwhile, had befriended the new boys, and with the money he'd saved up over the winter, he bought himself a pair of white pants and a short-sleeved silk shirt, and after begging a thousand different ways with the dashing youths he managed to get himself a sailor's cap. When he strolled out onto the square in his new get-up, his power-ful, well-proportioned body could make a young girl's heart flutter and her thoughts race – at least from afar. Yakup and I would exchange only quick hellos before he went off to join the new boys, and the girls would introduce him. They would play cards in the gazino and because he won more than he lost, he always had money in his pocket.

That summer we only went over to Spoon Island once. And that was with Odisya and his crew. Four Greek boys. With a fake smile he told them about the things we had done together the year before, but without affection. He made it sound foolish. I could see from the pained smile on Yakup's face that he, too, now thought it foolish, and that he found it distasteful to even speak about it.

Odisya's friends split their sides laughing.

With their Greek tangos, they chased all our Robinsons off our desert island along with the air of Robinson; they were rowdy enough to reduce the Portuguese pirate to tears. I kept thinking of how I had kissed Odisya. I kept peeling the skin off my lips.

The Hairspring

. . .

"How many minutes left?"

Clearly confused, he said:

"Till what?"

I looked at him, surprised.

"Till we get out of here, my dear," I said.

"Oh . . ."

Then he pulled a good-sized silver watch out of his pocket. Prying his eyes away from the blackboard, he looked down at it. He seemed calm, and a little afraid:

"Seventeen minutes . . ."

The spring afternoon came into the classroom in waves; flies were mating on the broad classroom windows, paying the botany teacher no heed. He was talking to us about seeds. They seemed to float in the thick, white light around us.

A sharp poke from behind. I spun around to hear someone say:

"How much time left? Ask him."

"You ask him. I already did."

The voice behind me:

"You beast."

I turned to the pensive boy beside me and said:

"Celil, *efendi*, my good man, I was wondering if you could tell me how much time is left?"

My friend was about to ask me again, "how many minutes until what?" But looking into my eyes he made the connection and pulled out his good-sized watch. With great reluctance, he said:

"Two minutes."

Every class went like this. Because he was the only one with a watch. Over the course of every lesson, he would take his timepiece out of his vest pocket. And then, in that deep, hoarse voice of his, he'd say:

"Ten minutes . . . Five minutes, twenty minutes, time's up . . ."

Lessons back then lasted fifty minutes. Once, I heard him calling out to the back: "Forty-five minutes!" There was shame in his voice that day, and exasperation.

But he was as punctilious about this duty as he was about his studies. Only during long breaks do I remember him looking at his watch without an audience. Though sometimes, as a lesson drew to a close, his thin and beautiful face would pale as his weary eyes went heavy with sleep. He would look down at his watch then, too.

After that first time, I never had to ask him again; he would just tell me.

One by one my hopes of going up to the next class were dashed. My heart was bitter and sad. In geometry class, where I didn't understand a thing, I never asked him for the time and neither did any of the others. Even the lazy students applied themselves. There was no time to ask for the time. I was pretty much the only one who dozed off. I could almost feel the steam rising up from my melting brain.

We were in geometry class, going over and over which factor went with which variable, and I just couldn't factor in any of it! I was stuck, and I turned to my friend.

There was something quick and bright about his sun-tanned face. I nudged him with my shoulder almost as if by accident. He turned and smiled at me. His eyes narrowed in on the angle on the blackboard.

"So it's like this," he said, "the outer angle of this triangle is equal to the two combined angles in this triangle because . . ." and he stopped.

He didn't want to make me feel bad, forcing his knowledge of geometry on me, and he said:

"I'll explain it later. Let's see what time it is."

His thick, long fingers plucked his watch out from his vest pocket with an uncanny ease. He cast his sad eyes over the face of his watch. They were fixed there for some time. Clearly he was still trying to work out the equation.

I was restless. The teacher was now looking at both of us. Then suddenly my friend turned to look at me. His eyes were swimming with anguish.

"I suppose I forgot to set it. It's not running."

He tried winding it. But the hairspring kept slipping. Crestfallen, he said:

"The hairspring's broken."

I didn't think anything of it, and for the first time I actually paid attention in geometry class. It was fun.

We had religion after geometry. The teacher had a way of speaking that bored us to death. He was an old man with a voice that was even older, and his passion for the subject had long since disappeared. But religion was a class where we could relax, because we never listened to that dull and mind-numbing voice. His examples were no good and the comparisons he concocted either had little or nothing to do with the topic.

Soon everyone was asking my friend for the time, whispering from near and far. Hearing them, he said, "The hairspring's broken." In the back row there was a student we didn't know very well. He was probably repeating the year. Or maybe he was our age, but he looked like an old man. The way he talked and the way he smoked reminded us of those strange men we saw in the neighborhood coffee houses; he was from the streets. He gave off those dark desires. When he called out from the back, his voice was rough, even unbridled. Or maybe he was trying to bring the poor teacher back to life:

"Damn, Celil! How many minutes left, for the love of God . . ."

My friend blushed bright red. I could see sorrow in his face, but also rage and loathing. He turned around and stared at the brute in the back without saying a word. I'm sure the brute would have beaten him to a pulp if the teacher had been the sort of man who would let a brute beat a boy who wouldn't hurt a fly. But the teacher was not that sort of man. With a kindly smile on his sallow face, he said:

"Celil, *efendi*, my son, could you have a look at your watch? I would also like to know how much longer I must wait until I can leave."

Ashamed, Celil stood up:

"Sir, the hairspring on my watch is broken."

Silence from the back. And then a shout:

"Boooo . . . The hairspring's broken . . . Go, hairspring Celil, go . . . Hairspring! Hairspring!"

Then there were cries from the back and the front:

"Hairspring! Hairspring!"

I never imagined that the nickname would stick, and neither did my friends. But even before he left the classroom, Celil himself seemed to know.

Within days, no one even remembered what his real name was. Even I wasn't sure what to call my sad-eyed friend: Celil or Hairspring.

I couldn't call him Celil because everyone else in the class called him Hairspring. And for the same reason, I couldn't call him Hairspring.

When they called him by that name, he would lower his head and do his best to ignore them; but on the second or third time, he'd turn to face them, calmly, furiously. But he wouldn't say a word.

■   ■   ■

It was the last class of the day. My friend stood up to help a friend with his work. On his desk there was a clean copy of a letter he'd been scribbling out since the beginning of class. Though I knew it was a tasteless thing to do, I read the letter out of the corner of my eye, as if my friend had never left.

Dearest Father,

I received your letter dated the 8th of this month. I can't tell you how happy I was to hear from you. The weather here has been excellent. Though yesterday clouds covered the sky, and it rained buckets. The Nilüfer plain was so beautiful in the rain. The entire plain stretches out in front of my window. In the mornings it's covered in mist, and it reminds me of the sea, and I think of Gemlik (that's where Celil was from) and I long to see you. I'm studying hard like you told me to. But father, if I may, I need to ask a favor of you. You know the watch you gave me on our journey to school. It's broken. You know the metal piece inside . . . what's it called, that curly steel bit inside? Well, that's broken. If someone is going that way next week I'll give them the watch. The school is full of clocks. I don't even need a watch. You can have it repaired and use it yourself. Love to you and mother and waiting for good news from you, my father.

Your son,

Celil

A Useless Man

. . .

I've been feeling odd lately. I prefer to keep myself to myself, and I don't want anyone knocking on my door, not even mailmen, the nicest men in the world. But I'm happy enough with my neighborhood. What if I told you I hadn't left it in seven years? Or that none of my friends know where I am? For seven years now, I haven't strayed beyond these four streets, except to walk down to Karaköy at the end of each quarter, to collect the rent from our store.

There are three parallel streets, and one that cuts across, and then there is my street, cut off from all the others and so short and narrow you might not even consider it a street. I have named the other streets One, Two, Three, and Four, in order of importance. But my street doesn't have a number. I just couldn't bring myself to do it.

A milkman lives on the ground floor of my building, and there are two carpenters across the street. I'd never been to a carpenter before. I'd always wondered how they got by. The ones on my street never stop working. They remind me of the gulf between me and other people: in forty years I haven't once needed a carpenter, that's just the way it is. It always surprises me when an Istanbullu actually goes to a carpenter. But who knows how many carpenters are doing business in this city of ours?

Once out of bed, I head straight for the café. It's a clean and tidy place with seven or eight tables, with customers who come and go without so much as a word, unless they retire to the corner to play King or Bezique or chess. The owner is a French-Jewish lady. The nicest woman in the world.

"Bonjour Madame," I say the moment I step inside.

"Bonjour Monsieur. Comment allez-vous?" she says.

I give all the right answers. But she knows better. She gives me what I think are honeyed words in French. I only understand a few. When I need to, I throw in the odd *oui*, and then a few *non*s to balance out the *oui*s. We get on really well. She tucks a French magazine under my arm and I sit down to look at the pictures. I jot down a few new words to look up in the dictionary when I get home, and when I read the magazine the next morning I say, *Goodness, who would have thought it?*

The madame: "Un cappuccino?"

Me: "Of course."

Then I throw down a *c'est ça* to keep it going in French. The lady is really pleased. She starts explaining how to make a cappuccino, in German.

And I listen.

Toward eleven I climb up the little street to the tramway line, turn left, and in just five steps I'm in front of a bookstore where I buy a few more illustrated French magazines. Stepping out with the magazines under my arm, I hurry back to my street. Ah! Such relief once I'm there. The people here are different, nothing like the ones near the tramway line. They scare me.

These days I'm hardly ever hungry, but there's a man who makes tripe soup in our neighborhood. He's an honest man and he makes good soup, and his place isn't anything like those filthy tripe soup restaurants in other parts of the city. His soup's as white as snow and he serves it in antique bowls.

"You like it seasoned, Mansur Bey?"

"Yes Bayram, I would," I say.

Maybe he's called Bayram or maybe Muharrem, but for me every man who sells tripe soup is called Bayram.

"Should I throw in a little vinegar and garlic, Mansur Bey?"

"Not today. It upset my stomach the other day, gave me gas. Have your waiter go fetch a lemon. Give it a quick squeeze of lemon instead."

"But we've saved the other half of the lemon we got for you the other day."

"Really?"

I was as happy as a child to hear about that half lemon. And Bayram was like a child, happy that I was happy and happy that he'd set the half lemon aside for me.

"Should I squeeze out the full half lemon, Mansur Bey?"

"Squeeze it dry, Bayram! Let's have it extra sour."

After finishing my extra sour soup, I go back up to my little apartment. With my French dictionary beside me, I fall asleep before I have even started translating the captions in the French magazine I bought earlier that day. I wake up at exactly four-thirty. Then I go out for a stroll. I leave my building, turn right, cross Street Number One and hurry along the sidewalk left of the tramway line before I dive into Street Number Two, which is parallel to Street Number One.

It's a narrow, seedy street. Caked with mud. There's a bar on the right, then a real estate agent, then a restaurant. I always get the feeling they serve forbidden fruit with their food. The same sad women go there every night with the same strange men; they could be eating frogs, or mice, or crows, or cats, or dogs, or even humans. I'm at the head of my street now.

I'm just passing by. I turn to my right to say hello to the woman who sells dried fruit on the street. "Hello, sir," she says. She has the most exquisite eyes. I hesitate before I turn right . . . Why?

I'll explain. Now this happened on one of my evening strolls. When most people go out for a stroll, they will pause now and again, if not to look into someone's eyes or a shop window, then just to take in their surroundings. Such things are beyond me. As I approach the street in question I begin to walk faster, eyes glued to the ground – all this to give the impression that it angers me to have to walk through it all. Why? Well let me explain.

The truth, sir, is that a true devil of a little Jewish girl lives in a house on that street, with a face that older ladies would describe as all in place (though she does have a spot in one eye, but what's the harm in that?) and gargantuan breasts that undulate in dark olive waves beneath her low-cut dress and hands plump enough to set a hazelnut on top. She sits at a window with winged shutters, absently sewing. But sometimes she lingers at the front door for hours, looking up and down the street, striking up conversations with every man who wanders by. Her full and strong legs keep her firmly on the ground, but olive-skinned Jews are the most beautiful of them all, and, oh, if only I could kiss those legs, just once.

Now, one day when I found myself ambling down that infamous street, the Jewish girl was at her door and the carpenter was standing at his door, which was just opposite. As I made to pass between them, the carpenter stepped out into the street, planting himself square in front of me.

"I've had enough from you – do you hear? You come by here one more time, I'll sock you in the eye."

From that day on I was tormented by the desire to walk down that street again. Oh the palpitations I suffered struggling to stifle that desire on my next few evening strolls. I knew the carpenter's threats weren't empty – he would come straight out and punch me in the eye! Oh what difficult days those were. For years I forced my heart to shut down from the moment I sensed the first flutter. For days my heart wouldn't allow so much as an extra beat. I'd check it: always sixty-three, always sixty-three, though sometimes it might drop to sixty-two. "It should settle into its normal rhythm when you're walking," a doctor friend of mine told me. But I couldn't just stop in the middle of the street and take my pulse! But I could sit down and relax and order a coffee and, throwing a glance left and right to see if anyone happened to be looking, I could discreetly pull out my watch to check: sixty-three. Even if a woman looked me in the eye, even if the price of oranges jumped from five *kuruş* to twenty-five, I refused to be moved. If they were selling for five, I'd eat them; if the price had gone up to twenty-five then it was goodbye to oranges. So back in the days when Street Number Three was a no-go area, like the rest of Istanbul, my evening strolls weren't so pleasant. I was trapped inside two streets. But I was never bored. In fact it was a quiet neighborhood, quiet but also vibrant. How could a Levantine-Jewish neighborhood not be vibrant? The Jews especially. What wonderful, warm, vibrant people. The neighborhood Jews weren't from the rich cut of society, and I'd no business with the rich anyway. When the local orange seller – that's Saloman – got more than forty *kuruş* out of me, he was the loveliest man in the world. When his oranges were too expensive and I didn't buy them, he didn't throw me dirty looks when I walked away or grumble when I offered him an impossible price. But just the opposite – he knew that I had every right.

It's evening. I know it is when the lady shuts the wooden blinds over her patisserie windows. There's a soft yellow light inside. She's switched on the electricity. Salomon puts a candle on his crate of oranges and the man who sells salted bonito plugs in a three hundred watt bulb. He slices red onions; they are the color of cyclamen and they shimmer as alluringly as lipstick or nail polish. Salted bonito! They conjure up the inner thighs of a voluptuous, olive-skinned Greek woman!

When ladies of the night want to be left alone, they step out of the *meyhane* with their misfortune and slip into my street to sidle up to me. Oh my miserable street!

There are two *meyhane* with live Turkish music on Street Number One. Taxis idle outside while drivers and prostitutes wander between the cars. Someone once told me that car antennae aren't really lightning rods put there to take a sudden bolt, but I was still fooled when I first saw them, the bright metal rods flashing white like lightning in the rain.

That tiny little tail on the back of an enormous beast of an automobile; I love that menacing and maniacal twitching. In the rain I stop in front of my tripe soup restaurant, pull my hat down over my ears and watch with what I imagine must be baleful eyes the people passing, and I pretend I have just been dropped into this neighborhood from a distant land without women, and am now searching for the one with whom I can share my sorrows.

Ten minutes later a man much older than me walks past. He's a burly fellow with a gray moustache, and though he has a full head of hair, it's gone gray. A driver spots him and says:

"Hey there. What's up?"

"Hello there, boys," he says.

Then he rattles off a few lines of dusty verse. When he's moved on, a driver says:

"He's an educated man, but twisted. Has a weakness for the young ladies. The younger and more wretched the better . . . What a fool!"

The educated man heads for the nightclub across the street. A little later, I head in after him. He walks toward the musicians and sits down right in front. He's a clean, well-dressed man, his hands, his hair, and his moustache are immaculate. He can't be more than fifty. There are one, two, three, four, five women in his booth. The sugar daddy levels his eyes on the youngest. They have her order him a drink and they bring him a pomegranate cooler with four or five drops of rubbing alcohol. They bring him one more. The man calls out to a coy girl with sweet round eyes and whispers into her ear before he begins to drop off. He falls asleep, his elbow propped on the table, but every now and then when the violinist in dark glasses strikes up a solo in a screeching that blends perfectly with the band, cutting through the soft chatter of the women, he moans, "Allah, Allah." The waiter Bekir told me how he rests his head on the chest of the girl he'll eventually leave with and how until then he sleeps there and weeps and sings and recites verse. Never more than these five things (for example, he never laughs). Then he goes back to sleep. Now he's deaf to the cries of the infamous brute from who knows which part of town, who flashes into the joint like lightning and screams at I don't know whom; he's still fast asleep when the *meyhane* proprietor – who hails from the Black Sea – moves in on two gangsters, throws them into the street and smashes the window front of a rival club. Some nights he even misses the young goliath who barges into the place with the rain and the snow, and (out of courtesy, perhaps, or just to make himself look important) sets up one of the chairs reserved for the tired, old singers to button up the trousers of a plump horn player, whose cheeks and neck and hair and moustache and coat collar are all soaked in sweat, who then proceeds to produce the most god awful screech on his thin little horn. The horn player is the last act with the band. He comes out around eleven, heaving his body about on two thick, short, fat legs. He takes off his velvet coat, tosses it in a corner of the room and salutes the blind violinist. The drummer whispers something to the blind violinist who cuts off the horn player's salute. And the zither player's taut, freshly shaved and alum-smeared face, hardly visible behind the singer, suddenly collapses into a million crinkles. The horn player sits down. Shouldn't there be buttons on his pants? Or have they popped off because he's so fat? The tassels on his green scarf dangle out of his fly. Some notice and laugh and the nightclub proprietor signals to him with a wink and a nod. Embarrassed, the horn player stands up, turns his back to the audience, takes a few moments to adjust his pants, sits back down, looks around the room, then pulls a cigarette case out of his pocket. It seems like he might roll a cigarette – but no, he pulls a reed out of one of his horns and puts it away. Then he takes out another one, surely the best one, or rather he pretends to be taking the best one out just for this night. That's when I always leave.

I haven't been anywhere else in Istanbul for seven years apart from this street. I'm afraid. I'm worried that I might get beaten up if I go further afield, or robbed, or lynched, and who knows what else – just the thought of leaving these streets fills me with confusion. Anywhere else, and I feel out of my depth. Everyone looks so frightening. I wonder who they all are, these people on the streets. The city is so huge, and everyone's a stranger. Why do they even make these cities to pack in this many people, when people don't like each other anymore? I just don't understand. Is it so that people can deceive and humiliate and murder each other? How can it be that so many strangers would wish to live in the same space?

If nothing else, a neighborhood is still a neighborhood. My shop could burn down, and I could go hungry. But somehow I have confidence that the man who sells me tripe soup with lots of lemon every afternoon will serve me until I die. And Saloman will keep handing me a bruised orange or two when I pass by, and to the half-dressed Jewish children on the street. My clothes might be old and ragged by then, they might not let me in, but the lady will still serve me a coffee at the door.

These are pipedreams, I know, but they show you how much I love my neighborhood. I don't want to see anyone else anymore, most particularly old acquaintances. Sometimes I run into one of them passing through my neighborhood.

"So finally! So this is where you've been hiding, is it?"

I lower my head and look down as if to say, what's the problem with that?

"People always said you could have ended up anywhere . . ."

The former friend will add:

"But damn it, you're still drifting, aren't you?" It's not about giving up the idle life, it's about giving up altogether, but I can't explain that to him. Some say:

"I know the deal, you rascal. You're chasing someone . . ."

The truth is, I've even stopped chasing after myself. But I still love that dark Jewish girl, the carpenter's friend, the one with the dark spot eyes, and the voluptuous hands. I can only dream of the other warm and sweet-scented corners beyond her legs.

Yesterday I decided for no reason to venture outside the neighborhood. I went to Unkapanı and then up to Saraçhane. Istanbul had changed so much since I'd last seen it. I was dumbstruck. But enjoying myself, none-theless.

Clean asphalt, broad avenues . . . What a splendid aqueduct – from a mile away, it looked almost like the Arc de Triomphe from a whole mile away! The Gazanfera? Madrasah just beside it: so bright and white and charming. I visited one park after another, to take refuge under the trees. And as I wandered fearfully through the city, I saw people, people every-where. I walked as far as Kıztaşı. I started down the hill from Fatih. Now I was in Saraçhane. I looked up and saw workmen on the top of a building they were demolishing. There used to be a hamam around here. That must be the building they were tearing down. I felt an overwhelming desire to go to a hamam.

Well, it seems there's no harm in saying it, seeing that I've already embar-rassed myself enough: I hadn't washed in seven years. In all that time it never even crossed my mind. But now I was itching, a terrible itching all over! I thought I had fleas. So I went into the hamam and I washed, oh how I washed! I washed off all the years of caked filth. I felt much better when I was done. But the sweat, so much sweat! Everywhere I rubbed I was sure to peel off bits of skin, grease, grime, or whatever it was. I was shocked at how much grease and grime a human being could carry. My skin was positively caked with it.

I left the hamam and got on the tram, thinking that I'd go home and then back out to Teşvikiye and the surrounding districts. But once my head hit the pillow I fell asleep and slept for a full twenty-four hours. I woke up the next day at two and hurried out for a bowl of tripe soup.

"God praise, Mansur Bey, you look the picture of perfect health," Bayram said.

I couldn't tell him I'd been to a hamam. I asked for soup without garlic. Then I went for my stroll. I was in Maçka by nightfall. A different world entirely. Back home I promised myself I wouldn't leave my neighborhood for another seven years, but it didn't happen that way. Something was making my head spin, and for the next two days my life made no sense. Can you guess what I got to thinking? That I'd sell our store and my apartment. And you know that nightclub I was telling you about, the one with the live music? And that girl working outside taking orders, you know the one with the small forehead. Well, I'd take her as my lover. And a year after that I'd die.

I'd jump on a Bosphorus boat one day, taking my seat on one of those benches at the back, and somewhere near Arnavutköy or Bebek, I'd stand up, check to make sure no one was looking and, if I was alone, I'd climb over the railing and jump into the sea.

Papaz Efendi

.   .   .

The church was just across the street from us. It was hemmed in by pines, which at twilight would sink into shadow, leaving the brick walls of the church to glow red and hot against a dark blue sky. Often we'd see a crow or a poet seagull landing beside the cross on the roof, which, lacking a bell tower, had been restored many hundreds of times by Greek master builders of the Orthodox faith (or others oblivious to it), and at times like these it seemed more like the home of a Byzantine feudal lord than a church. It wasn't an ugly building, but it wasn't pretty either. It had only one main dome; where there should have been smaller domes, there were holes and crenels that looked like gutters. By day it all looked rather crude and tired, but when the evening blues and greens turned dark enough to seep into the color of the tiles, the church looked so close you almost thought you could reach out and grasp the cross on the top and pull away the entire tableau, without so much as frightening a bird away, to stencil it onto a dark blue background in your notebook or hang it on your wall, to savor forever after. That's how the church looked to me on May evenings. As a child I was always trying to get those evenings onto the page, perhaps I lamented the fact I wasn't a painter or a child putting stickers in his notebook. The bell tower was in the front yard, though you couldn't really call such a thing a bell tower. It had two bells: a big one that rang on the days someone died and a small one that rang to announce ferryboat and prayer times to the village. I first saw Papaz Efendi sitting cross-legged with a black hat in his lap on a board between two pines, a little behind the bells. His beard was pitch-black, and so were his eyes. He was wearing a raw silk shirt that he seemed to have slipped into without using his hands. It shimmered in the sunlight. The greasy tufts of hair hanging over his forehead gave him the look of an unruly child.

"Hello, sir."

"Hello, Papaz Efendi."

"How are you, sir? We're neighbors, I believe."

"That's true."

Whenever he flashed his bright teeth beneath his black beard, he suddenly looked less Orthodox, less Byzantine. Having shed his churchman's mask, he would take on the delightful aspect of a workman relishing a meal.

"Tell your mother I'll be tending the garden over the winter."

"I'll tell her." And I did.

Early next morning I found Papaz Efendi tilling the garden with a spade. His long raincoat hung over an apple tree like a scarecrow. He had pale, muscular arms and long, white fingers that kept a firm grip on the spade. Leaning over, he picked up a handful of dirt:

"I love the earth for its quiet, its humility, its passion, its peace. The earth is the source of all life. How could anyone be more alive than the earth? That's why they say we're made of the earth."

"So you're a philosopher, Papaz Efendi?"

"Oh I'm not a philosopher and I'm not a priest. I'm a human being without any earth to call my own. Or home, or religion."

"Religion?"

"In a way, absolutely. But if there's a God, I suppose He created us to live. On those terms, I can accept Him."

He paused.

"But let's forget all that. Think of the earth . . ."

"How old are you?" I asked.

"Sixty-three."

"What?"

He stood straight and tall: There wasn't a pinch of spare flesh or flab on his body; well proportioned and straight as a rail, nothing he didn't need.

"Heavens, that's impossible. You don't look a day over forty."

"I live to eat. I'll drink my fair share of wine if it's around, and you'll never see me without a cigarette hanging from my lips. I'll eat leaves and birds and if there's nothing else, I'll eat the earth – but never human flesh. It's my stomach – I have an iron stomach. But I don't eat much, just the amount I need to get the gears turning. I'll never overindulge, but I like my food and drink. It keeps me young. And another thing – I never listen to what others have to say about me: 'The papaz drinks rakı, he gets drunk, he chases after girls, he laughs too much.' That's what they say. Well, let them talk. To me it's mindless chatter, nothing more. I've always wanted to make something of my life but I never did. I never gambled, no, I never went that far. Of course, there's a part of me that wishes I had. When I was young there was a time when I ate nothing but bread and onions, and if a pretty girl walked past me, I'd whinny like a colt."

"I don't believe you, Papaz Efendi."

"That's the way I was, sir. And why not? Because I'm a priest? I'm in love with beautiful things: beautiful women, good wines, and grass and trees and flowers and birds – everything that's beautiful."

And he spoke beautiful Turkish.

"You'll have to excuse me now. But I'll see you soon." And with a soft thud he drove his spade into the moist red earth.

"Here, have a look," he said. "How is this any different from a handful of gold? What's gold to us anyway?"

He leaned over and pulled up a tuft of curled couch grass and looked me in the eye and smiled, showing me his sturdy teeth.

"Our teeth are strong because we don't have gold, because we love the earth and are nourished by it. It's a blessing not to have gold. If we did we'd have long since died of overindulgence. Our livers could never have taken it."

When Papaz Efendi's tussle with our little garden was over, he stood there like a man who'd won a lover's quarrel, compassionate and proud; and there, bedecked with flowers, was the beauty who'd submitted to his will: the radiant earth. Every tree had the perfect number of branches. Not a trace of unwanted couch grass on the ground. The tomato vines had grown high.

As he surveyed the garden's middle rows – the cucumber flowers and the newly budding yellow squash – he puffed on a cigarette, his reward for a job well done.

I watched him from my window: he was sitting on a rock eating sunflower seeds and flicking the shells over the great mounds of earth, marveling at their flight. It was a late May afternoon and heavy lightning clouds had gathered in the sky like mist. He saw me and looked over his garden.

"Well, what do you think?"

I looked out.

"Magnificent, Papaz Efendi. You've won," I said.

He thought for a moment.

"I am a soldier of the seed. The soil is my battlefield. Defeat would sully my name. Come on down."

He was standing tall in the garden, leaning against his spade, and he seemed to me the spitting image of the shepherd from the Holy Book.

"You look like a victorious general," I said.

He smiled.

"Pasha Papaz Aleksandros," he said.

And he picked up a handful of moist red earth and rubbed it into his beard.

"Iron, magnesium, phosphorus, calcium, everything's here," he said. "But I know seeds. They're little granaries, little eggs. But this thing, the earth, well that's something else, something I could never understand. A scientist can analyze it and tell us there's so much of this and so much of that. But seeds, well there's no problem providing everything they need: scent, color, vitamins, minerals, iron, phosphorus, arsenic, sugars and, who knows what else?"

"Is that all? What about sunshine and the rain?"

"They're less important, somehow. Maybe because they're too proud. Rain makes us beg and pray for it, and when it comes pouring down from the sky, we rejoice and give our thanks to the Lord. And while the sun shimmers all day long in the sky, the earth says, *I have something for every one of you. You can't live without me. Without me all your efforts would be smoke.* All winter the earth lies and waits silently beneath our feet, soiling our boots and our clothes. It's pitch-black, or the color of ash, or yellow, or dark red, or lifeless mud or clay. Then with spring it releases unbridled joy. It showers us with its bounty, and the festival begins: clover spreads across the pastures. Poppies and daisies cover the hilltops. Even the straw brooms seem to smile. The earth gives without asking for anything in return. It's generosity, sheer generosity! And then, after it has showered us with so much joy, it begins to recede. It decays and gives birth. It decays and gives birth. Women are of the earth, that much is clear. Mother Earth. Mother

Earth! There's a little earth in every female. Perhaps men are children of the sun. Perhaps we're made of air and water. But women – they're made of the earth."

He opened his hand and let the soil fall over his eggplant seedlings.

"Have you ever heard me sing?"

"No," I said.

"I have a beautiful voice. You should hear me sing. When I sing my prayers, it's not Jesus and his father I'm praising. It's the earth. You should hear me. These Byzantine dirges are dreadful. They're painful and they're false. The world they paint is an illusion. It's a kind of slow madness, full of longing, and grief. Lust and enslavement. But I sing them differently. Everything changes when I sing with the earth in mind. The island has two beautiful voices. One is mine. No one doubts that. The other belongs to the fisherman Antimos. Have you ever heard him sing?"

"No, I haven't," I said.

"I'm sure you have, but you weren't really listening. He sings when he's weaving or mending his nets. You can't understand the beauty of his voice if you're too close. It's nothing but a faint echo. He sings so softly you hardly hear him. Would you like to hear him? Take a rowboat out to sea when he sings beside the kiosk on the shore. Row out for ten minutes or so and stop in the middle of the sea. That's when you'll hear the fisherman's song. When you're just beside him you can't really hear him, but no matter where else you go in the sea you'll hear him. And so clearly that . . . Then listen to him for a while. At first you'll feel restless, overwhelmed. Then start rowing swiftly, moving farther out from shore. Then even farther! Don't be afraid. The voice will find you. And from the moment you stop hearing, to the moment you begin rowing toward it again, you will know. Maybe you've gone out just to catch a fish or two. But when you look into the sea and see its fish and the light on the water and the lapping waves splashing all around you, you will understand – this song is not of God, but of man. The fisherman might think he's singing to God, but he's not – he's singing for the sea. He's eighty years old, and he's never hurt a soul. He's spent his life weaving nets and taking his sustenance from the sea. If he didn't fish for two days, he'd go hungry, but for seventy years he's fished every day, catching enough to buy his daily bread. Nothing more. He's found a treasure that offers him the same bounty every day and nothing more. He never deprives others of their fair share. I can't tell you how much I love the song of thanks and praise that he sings for the sea. In church, I sing for the earth. But it's a sinner's lament. I earn my living peddling a drug that has deceived humankind for centuries. I am the opium for those who can't sleep. Who knows what my people would do if they knew that every time I don my golden robe, I pray only for the earth. They'd leave me and I'd go hungry, hungry!"

He scooped up another handful of earth and said:

"I say my prayers for the earth. Listen to me and to the fisherman, too. He sings for the depths of the sea. He's a holy man who has found truth, though he doesn't know it. Eighty years old and in his whole life he's only ever hurt a fish! But I'm a clever sinner. I envy fishermen and farmhands who till the soil. Only them and no one else . . ."

Once I heard Papaz Efendi preach, and I listened to the fisherman Antimos, both close and from a distance, and though the Byzantine litany remained a mystery to me, the songs gnawed away at me like dark worms, for days on end.

The two voices were always ringing in my ears and on sleepless nights I would listen to them through my window. I'd fall so deeply into myself I could hear the flow of blood in my veins.

When Papaz Efendi tilled the soil: now that was something worth seeing. His joy seemed boundless. The only priest-like thing about him left was his beard, as black as the beards of the youngest men of the earliest race of man. The villagers didn't take well to Papaz Efendi, but he never begrudged them. He'd have long and friendly chats with anyone. He paid no heed to their gossip. Once, in the coffeehouse, he said:

"Now who's the one saying I'm a ladies' man?"

When no one said a word he looked directly into the eyes of the man who'd stirred up the gossip.

"Enjoying women is like breathing, and how can we live without breathing, my friends?"

One moonlit night I saw Papaz Efendi sipping cold rakı on the top of the island with a group of Greek men and women celebrating around a roasted lamb. His dark mohair frock tunic was tucked into his belt. It glistened in the moonlight as he danced with a plump young girl. In one hand he held her little hand and a pure white napkin that looked like mastic; in his other hand he held his glass of rakı; and every so often he stopped to mop her brow.

In the winter I'd go out to the island on Saturdays now and again. I'd find Papaz Efendi in the garden. He'd show me his spinach and onions.

"You shouldn't come out here alone. It's cold. You need someone to make you salad," he said. On the days I wasn't alone in our house, and Papaz Efendi saw the reflection of a woman in the window, he would flash me a smile, baring a row of strong teeth, and it was like the sun shimmering off the sea on a summer afternoon.

Papaz Efendi passed away last summer. He died of liver failure. His stomach was the size of a balloon.

"It's cirrhosis. I shouldn't have contracted something like this. I don't believe in illness. The pain's only in my head."

"What's happened, Papaz Efendi? There's a rumor going around."

"Don't pay any attention to that. I did, and now I'm dying. That dishonorable villager slandered me. It's a lie. You have to believe me. But maybe I'll survive. I'll get through this one, too."

But he didn't, and he died. Papaz Efendi was only guilty of leading on a silly girl. Three days before he died I saw him in a countryside café. His face was pale. This was the day I noticed the pockmarks under his beard. But she was still young, still beautiful. He'd lost a lot of weight but his stomach was clearly bloated.

"They started talking about it the other day," he said. Then he pointed to a bright young girl with sun-kissed legs.

"Now if all this gossip had to do with a girl like that I wouldn't feel such a pain in my heart."

"But I thought you never gave such gossip any notice, Papaz Efendi."

"It's gotten to me this time, and now it's under my skin," he said. "Why are people so obsessed with each other's lives? I suppose with death knocking at the door it's harder to bear. Otherwise I wouldn't mind. But who knows? Are they all just backstabbing fools and liars and thieves? Don't I know that they're all after each other's livelihood, their wives and their daughters? But I'm not like that. I have three more days, and I intend to spend them laughing, and loving Mother Earth, and marveling at beautiful girls."

Three days later, Papaz Efendi was dead.

The Valley of Violets

. . .

My friend was lost in thought. His head was resting in his gigantic hands. His half liter of wine stood half empty; his rank mackerel and rancid green beans were misery in still life; even someone who hadn't eaten in days would know that the food was somehow alive, mourning its own decay: a single bite was bound to bring on sharp stomach pangs. Abandoned food in second-rate tavernas looks so forlorn: I see traces of the same resignation in men who haven't chosen a mate and women who have not yet been chosen.

His name was Bayram: he was a big-boned man who spoke Turkish with an Albanian accent. Once upon a time he'd sold dried almonds that he turned back into fresh almonds with nitric acid and ash; after that he sold lottery tickets; then he was a driver, and for a while I suppose he was making a decent living, earning thirty or forty lira a day. That's when I met him. But old habits die hard: he still dressed like a mobster and he could still burn through a week's wage in a day. He hung out with the prettiest girls in the worst tavernas. Seher was one of them. She was incredibly tall. He had already moved in with her. I'd seen her in his car.

"Hey, my man," he'd say. "You mark my words, that one's a devil in disguise."

And he'd crack his whip over his horses and the wiry mares would shoot through the narrow streets like lightning. So Bayram was living with Seher then, and they got into all sorts of fights. Once there was even a stabbing. He was on the run for days but eventually they caught him. They put him away for seven or eight months. That's when Seher fell for an officer, she'd always had a thing for men in uniform. And then she stopped going to the taverna on Asmalimescit.

Bayram couldn't work after that. His spine stuck out like pack poles on a saddleless camel. He'd start drinking in the morning. And he was bent on finding Seher. One day he drew an enormous knife out from under his belt and slashed her side. But she didn't die. And she never told anyone who'd done it.

After she was released from the hospital she went back to the taverna but she refused to speak to Bayram. And that's what really got to him. She was tough and had him tied up like a workhorse. But time went by and they made up and Bayram sold his carriage and his mares. And Seher burned through all his money. She was literally breaking Bayram's back. By that time he was driving someone else's carriage for ten lira a day. He didn't like the people she spent time with. Eventually he lost his job driving the carriage and he went back to selling almonds.

I would find him drinking away his wages in the tavern; steeped in darkness, his face looking like a bombed-out European city. His eyes no longer flamed. The light had gone out of his chiseled face, the passion, too. And he had a harsh, dry cough. Some of the old luminosity came back when he was drinking, but the passion – it only returned when he headed out to kill Seher. Finding him in that pitiful state one night, I said:

"Bayram, my friend. What the hell's happened? This is crazy."

"Sit down," he said, and then he shouted, "Barba! Another bottle of wine!"

Barba brought us a bottle of Çavuş white and we got pretty drunk. At one point Bayram gave me the strangest look; he was on the verge of saying something but stopped himself. I didn't push him, but then he said:

"I love you like a brother, and you love me, right?"

"How could you think otherwise, Bayram?"

"So then would you take me home?"

"Sure. If you're that drunk," I said.

"No, not to my room," he said. "Home, home, my real home. I haven't been back in seven years."

"Seven years?"

He smiled.

"One morning seven years ago, I left," he said. "It was February and I had just turned twenty-one, but the waters in our stream were still as warm as a morning in spring, and the air was filled with the scent of violets. I set out for Beyoğlu with a bunch of flowers in my arms. I sold them in the Çiçekpasaj. I got nine lira for them. I hadn't tasted drink before that. And then I did. I'd been married for three years but I'd never tasted a woman who was done up and perfumed. After that I never went back home. I wonder if any of them are still alive. In all this time, I've never run into one of them. My dad was already an old man then. Then there's mother, and my wife and my two children, one a year and a half and the other just nine months. So I sold almonds, as you know, and you know the rest, too."

He called out to the proprietor:

"Barba! A bottle of red, but make it a full liter."

"Hold on, Bayram! You've had enough as it is."

I asked the old waiter how many bottles he'd drunk.

"I really don't know, brother," he said, "I'm not too good with this sort of thing. I've written it down here, everything he drinks, but I may be wrong . . ."

In a warm voice Bayram said:

"Bring us the wine, but I won't drink any."

But he had some all the same. Then I ordered another bottle. When we were back on the street I could barely stand, and Bayram was no better. We stopped off at the taverna on Asmalımescit and asked for Seher and the waiter Bekir. We were told they'd gone to the Hilltop, so we jumped in a car and sped off. Bayram kept muttering:

"I'll topple her down the hilltop."

Thank God Seher wasn't there. From there we set out on foot. It was damp and the wind was cold and pieces of icy cloud slid across the sky. From time to time the moon seemed more suspicious than usual. From time to time the driving wind was at our backs, and from time to time it pushed us back.

Suddenly we stopped and it was calm. A great old Ottoman house emerged from the night. We were in a cabbage patch; we had somehow stumbled over the garden walls. Bayram leading the way, we began descending into the darkness, trudging over the soft earth; the wind grew softer and softer and soon we were surrounded by thick, warm air. I could hear the sound of water. A soft light flowed from the huddle of buildings below. Dogs barked in the distance. We knocked on a door. A girl's voice on the stairs:

"Mother! Someone's at the door."

"Well go and open it. Grandpa must be back from the coffeehouse."

"I'm scared."

"What's there to be scared of?"

"There are two men out there."

"Don't be silly. Well then it must be Grandpa and Uncle Hasan."

The door opened, and a girl with blond hair and speckled blue eyes stared vacantly at Bayram's face. Then her luminous blue eyes were on me, looking me over. And she slammed the door shut.

"There are thieves at the door, Mom! Thieves, I swear to God, thieves!"

Then a woman was standing before us; her brow was pure white, her eyes were jet black and wide open in surprise, and she held her headscarf over her mouth. First she simply stood there, staring, then she pulled the headscarf away from her mouth, stepped back and said:

"Come in, gentlemen."

We went in. There was a stairwell just beyond the door. We hadn't gone up ten steps before we were at another door. We opened it. We were in a room with an iron stove, and a strong scent of children and linden flowers. We sat down on the divan as a low, round wooden table was set in the middle of the room and a round copper tray, sparkling with red streaks of light, was placed on top; pickles, cheese, jam and six hardboiled eggs sat on the tray. We sat around the table, and without saying a word we ate. While we ate a little boy opened the door, peered in, and then disappeared. The little girl attended to us while we ate and when we finished, the older girl returned, with her hair pulled back and her headscarf tied tightly around her forehead. She moved in and out of the room in silence, collecting the empty dishes from the tray. Then she opened the lid of a large chest, laid out blankets for two beds and left the room. Later she came with coffee. We went to bed without exchanging words. It was like we were angry with each other: frowning, we avoided each other's eyes.

When I awoke in the morning, Bayram was by the window smoking a cigarette. I sat down on the divan beside him and looked at the garden below, stretching out before us in the mist. On one side there was something like a greenhouse, covered in glass and wicker. I opened the window and breathed in the sweet scent of violets. The weather was warm, almost balmy. Soon the mist slowly rose and I could see the entire orchard: cabbages, flowers, parsley and lettuce all rearing up like horses. In the distance among the flowers there were other gardens, other warped, crooked buildings. The same vegetables, the same animals, the same bent and solitary structures filled the surrounding landscape, and everywhere the scent of violets. A swirling stream ran across the road. Did we cross it when we came to the house the night before? I couldn't remember getting my feet wet.

An old man came up behind us.

"Dad!" Bayram cried.

It was the first word uttered since the night before.

The old man turned to me and said, "Welcome home, my son."

Then an old woman brought us milk and said to the old man:

"Are you going to the market? Should I get the cart ready?"

The man looked at Bayram.

"Yes, I'm going, Mother!" Bayram said.

The old woman wiped away a tear waiting to run down her wrinkled cheek. It seemed that no one else was touched by Bayram's return.

Cabbages, leeks, red radishes, and spinach were loaded onto the carriage, and we piled in. Bayram's little girl turned up with a bursting bouquet of violets and gave them to me, and a woman with a face as yellow as a quince came running to the carriage with an armful of celery root. She threw them all into the carriage, lifting only her eyes to glance at Bayram. I looked at Bayram, but he didn't seem to notice. She watched the carriage until it disappeared from view. Bayram didn't stand until we had turned the corner. Then he cracked his whip over the white workhorse, turned, and snapped it back toward the woman who had been watching him disappear. We had turned the corner so we couldn't see the woman racing back home.

I could smell the violets, oh, and that wonderfully pungent scent of the celery root! I wasn't sure where we were going and didn't ask.

When we got to the market we jumped out of the carriage and the middlemen swarmed around Bayram.

"Back from military service? We thought you'd died, my man Bayram!" they cried.

"I'll be off then, Bayram," I said.

"Stop by some time."

I wandered along so many streets, down and up and then back down again until I ended up in Ortaköy.

I haven't been back to the valley of violets in nearly a year. I always said I was going but then I could never find it. But last year, one cold day in February, I found myself with a few friends in that same cabbage patch near Mecidiyeköy. The landscape before us opened onto a valley whose depth and mystery drew us toward it. I knew just where I was when I felt the soft earth under my feet, and over the soft earth we ran down into the valley. And the valley was so warm, so warm, and steeped in the scent of violet. We walked along the bank of the stream and saw Bayram hoeing a lettuce patch with a pick, his wife bent over the earth, collecting what I think was mallow. She turned to look at us. Bayram didn't remember me at first so I had to introduce myself to him.

As we traveled back up into the hills of Arnavutköy, passing along the edge of the garden, we could still smell the violets. We left a warm day in May to find February waiting for us like a whip.

The Story of a Külhanbeyi

. . .

The street was deserted. Where else would a raw cucumber like him get it on with his girl? The bar's a little further on. You can see the agency light reflected in its iron grill.

In the old days this was an Ottoman *han*, but now they rent by the room. It's more a prison than a *han*. There's this office next door. But no, that's the agency. You can buy a ticket to America there. But the main attraction is just opposite: the state factory. They make booze there. Man! Do they ever! Sometimes you just want to bang on that metal grate and scream, "Damn it, man! Can't you give me just one little taste?"

Ömer keeps an eye on people who go into the *han* and don't come out. Every day he listens to that horrible mash of languages pouring out through the agency's back window. It's bracing stuff. Even the curly blonde gets a little scared, though she should be used to it by now.

But now she is soothed by the harmonies of the *suma* factory: the beds, the slippers, and the strops; she can even hear the trembling whispers of desire – she likes them.

Ömer is sitting on a truck, inside a wreath of cigarette smoke. He is waiting for someone to leave but his slow and heavy gestures betray no anxiety. Though his shoulders are hunched, he keeps one a little higher, just in case. The shabby ends of his long pants dangle over the edge of the truck – it looks like he has no legs. A few people go into the *han*. A few go out. He listens to their footsteps crossing the long courtyard. He thinks of taking off, but then he stretches. Stretches and stretches until he feels as long as that dark and dusty courtyard. He can almost feel the footsteps in his chest. Now comes the worst of it: the ruthless, godless desires that come on with the drink. Hours go by and no one comes out.

The *han* has five floors, with a great courtyard in the middle. There are sunflower seeds and cucumber skins and paper wrappers scattered over the stone steps. But no matter how drunk a man gets, he always knows when it's a cherry pit jammed in the sole of his tattered shoe. That's just how it is. It's the season, my friend. The cherry season. Surely the *han* boys wouldn't be eating strawberries at this time of year! And what the hell's a strawberry seed, anyway?

Now, if I were Ömer, I'd check out that dark elevator that's been sitting idle there for years. When he gets to the second floor, he regrets not looking in. But it's too late to go back.

Not a single beam of light slips out onto the torn and dusty linoleum floor. That's good – it means everyone's asleep. Why not light a cigarette? His match hits the floor, leaving a little scratch in the dust. Like the wick of a dynamite stick, almost. Oh mother of God! What's become of us? he asks himself. This place gives him the creeps. Why in the world would anyone want to be here?

He tries every room on the third floor. A woman peers out through the sack that's been taped over the broken glass. Calling back into the room, she says:

"Careful, Hüsnü, there's a guard downstairs."

She stands erect and silent; Hüsnü must be doing the same. Isn't that why she stays there, eyeing the corridor?

"Hüsnü," she says. "Give me a cigarette."

He is three steps behind her. He hands her a cigarette. Then the matches. He waits. She takes them.

The woman says:

"Hüsnü, I'm leaving tomorrow. That's why I called you here. Did Hatice tell you?"

He comes three steps closer. With one stroke, he pushes the door open. As the darkness in the room collides with the darkness outside, she cries:

"Come to the pier tomorrow morning and we can talk there. If you don't come, I'll leave my clothes at the gazino."

She has stepped outside now, with Hüsnü. But Ömer doesn't understand a thing she's saying. Who is Hüsnü? Which Hüsnü? Which clothes, at which gazino?

The second room is locked. The man in the third room groans:

"Who's that? Who the hell's out there? You've got the wrong room, my friend."

The handle on the next door turns. A blinding shaft of light pins him to the doorsill. Man! This light is slicing right into his brain like a bullet.

There is a bed on the floor and an overturned strawberry basket in the corner. A plateful of onions, cucumbers, and bits of tomato, and a bottle of water beside it. Is it water? Two people are in the bed. One has graying hair. He can't see the other. Just a bit of leg peeping out from the covers. Smooth and slender. Olive-skinned. He imagines long black hair. Good, he can't see it!

What a powerful bulb! How many watts? A hundred? That hulking, graying man has pushed the tiny olive-skinned leg into a corner. That little bump under the covers is snoring. No – not snoring. Whistling. Wheezing, like the strops in a rakı plant. How beautiful is that? There's nothing revolting about it. Doesn't rakı make that sound when it passes through the alembic, and those zinc tubes? Something between a whistle and a snore? But no, it turned out not to be that little creature snoring under the yellow blanket: it is just a puppy, snatched from its pack. None of this is arousing. Well, just one thing: the protruding shoulder under the blanket. If he were not already slipping through the door and into darkness, he'd be pulling back that blanket. Kissing that shoulder. Facing the music! Maybe a matter for the switchblade. He turns to look but lets the idea go.

In the corridor he bumps into three young baker's boys. He doesn't argue with them because he has other things on his mind: rocky shoulder under the yellow blanket. The whiff of dust.

The boys retreat into their room. He hears the clink of coins . . . *Simit* sellers always slap down their coins when they count them. There's no other way to count the money made from *simits*. It's one thing to wet your thumb and index finger and flick through a wad of paper cash. But slapping down coins is what it sounds like: a slap. And then another. And another.

He joins his hands. Laces his fingers. Hits his knee. Slap. Slap. Slap! Then he looks up. Our Külhanbey is acting like a little child. What if someone sees? What is the difference between darkness and childhood? But he has no time for this. He is in love. He's broke. He leaps up the steps in fours, and now he reaches his floor.

"Hey, you in there!" he cries. "It's me. Wake up, you bastards!"

Doors open and close. Then silence. A woman appears from behind one of the doors. He stares. She goes back inside. Then an old woman opens another door. Ömer looks at her. She says:

"Come on, Ömer, get inside."

"You go, mother, just relax."

"You'll get cold, Ömer."

Oh, the way she speaks, a booming voice, like a man. What a woman! The mother of a Külhanbey!

"Mind your own business."

His mother stiffens. She closes the door.

Ömer turns toward the other door. On the other side of this door is the person he is waiting to see leave the *han*. He walks over and sits down. He puts his head on the mat. He drops off.

"Ömer, Ömer, get up!"

He stays silent as the tenant shakes him and sweeps him away, dragging him down the stairs. Now they are standing in front of the truck. She says:

"You have anything to say, Ömer?"

"Nah, what would I have to say, nothing!"

She presses two pale twenty-five notes into his hand. She has come into some cash, then. Ömer looks down at the money.

"Whore's money, man. Screw it," and he spits on the ground.

The streets of Galata are waking up to the smell of rakı.

The Little Coffeehouse

. . .

I came often in the summer to sit in the garden of this little coffeehouse, and so no one thought it strange when I walked in that evening through swirls of snow and an angry northwest wind. The coffeehouse was in a quiet and secluded neighborhood. The bare branches of the willow trees that made the garden so charming in the warm months were now coated with snow, as was the vine from which three or four dry leaves still dangled, and I was so entranced by the scene I had just glimpsed that I reached over to the misty window and rubbed a patch clear, and there it was again, that bright white glow rising from every root, and the air tinged with violet. Night fell so quickly that the violet was gone before the lights came on inside. As the proprietor set the loveliest of his tulip tea glasses on my table, he said, "It's beautiful here in the winter, too, isn't it?"

He gestured at the snow that had settled over his blue chrysanthemums. "If I knew the old men weren't going to grumble, I'd leave the lights off longer, but then, who knows, they might start snoring."

The lights in the coffeehouse had snuffed out the snowlight. I looked around me. There could not have been more than seven or eight others in the coffeehouse. The flames were licking the little lid of the stove whose right-hand side would soon, I knew, be molten red. Next to me were some men playing backgammon. For a while I watched them. And occasionally I would wipe a patch of the window clear, and press my forehead against the glass to gaze at the scene outside.

Leaving home that afternoon, I had been struck by the sudden silence, and by the great snowflakes falling into it: taken by the urge to walk, I turned away from the avenues that were certain to be crowded, and where I might run into friends; wishing for a place less frequented, where the snow might be left to accumulate untouched, I had boarded a tram and come here. But along the way the weather had worsened, the northwest wind had grown fiercer and the large, wet snowflakes had begun to mix with hail.

I turned to the proprietor.

"Do you have today's paper?" I asked.

He pressed a newspaper into my hand. Though my thoughts now turned to the day's rumors, I continued to dip in and out of the conversations around me. These were the usual desultory discussions about how hard it was to make a living. Now and again a door would fly open, sending in a great gust of wind, and a man would blow on his hands as he crossed over to the stove. Once he had warmed himself, he would find a perch somewhere, or lose himself to a daydream, or join two men who had been perfectly content playing backgammon by themselves, and, despite their protests, become their unwanted third.

A number of grave-faced middle-aged men joined the old men on the long divan. I was a long way away from them. I couldn't hear what they were saying, but I could see they were at peace. For the longest time they sat there in silence. And then a moment arrived when I realized that no one had come into the coffeehouse for quite some time. The proprietor's little clock was facing the other way so I couldn't read it. More time passed.

More people left. At last the proprietor turned his clock around for me. It was half past ten. I was feeling so drowsy that I couldn't summon the energy to get up and go. Sensing that I would be on my way soon, the proprietor said:

"If you live nearby, there's no hurry. We're open till one. Do you really think you could find a better place than this?"

"Oh, all right," I said. "Make me another tea. With a slice of lemon."

Just then a man came inside. He was blanketed in snow. Even his eyebrows and eyelashes were white. He walked over to the stove. Swept off the snow. Collapsed into a chair. He was young, this man, very young. The snow melted to reveal a round, white face.

All conversation stopped. The backgammon players in the corner slammed the wooden box shut and left. The silence grew deeper.

I examined the young man. He was sitting in a chair, staring straight ahead. The old men sat still and solemn on their sofa. In their eyes I could see a touch of malice. The proprietor was sitting in front of his stove, his head between his hands. It is a terrible thing to sit in a public space in silence. Ten minutes passed and still the fearsome silence continued.

The young man kept throwing his left leg over his right, and then his right leg over his left. He couldn't seem to make himself comfortable in that chair of his. From the waist up, he looked like a student at an exam. A student shifting in his chair and then looking up, to make sure the examiners hadn't seen his crossed legs beneath the table. One of his shoes was a scrap of old tire covered with red patches; he had tied it to his foot with a piece of string. On the other foot was an old gym shoe that gaped open like a fish, with its sole swinging.

The silence continued. I kept hoping for someone to say:

"The devil passed."

Or:

"A girl was born!"

And then we would all laugh.

But still no one spoke. Once again, I turned my gaze toward the new arrival. It was not his face that drew me now, but his forehead. It was blank and unlined. He wasn't wearing a jacket. Instead he wore a loose, collarless shirt, white lined with black. Over this he had wrapped a bulky, dirty white sweater, held together in the front with a hook needle.

By now my curiosity had got the better of me. I sat there, unable to move.

Just then the coffeehouse door opened and another man walked in. He went straight over to the old sages.

"He's called for you," he said. "His mind is still clear but I'd bet my life on it, he won't last till morning. He keeps going in and out. Ali Ağa, he's asked for you. And you, too, Sergeant Mahmut. And if you want, you can come, too, Hasan. He was very fond of you."

The three elders rose to their feet. Though they did not so much as glance at the young man seated by the stove, their eyes somehow managed to bore into him as they passed. It was as if they were deliberately looking away from him. He watched them go, his large eyes pleading.

The proprietor had not offered him so much as a glass of tea. When he came over to take my own glass, I said, "Make the poor boy some tea. You can put it on my tab."

The proprietor shut his eyes and opened them again, giving me the oddest look. Then he walked away, to get the young man his tea, I thought.

As he passed before him, the young man jumped to his feet. He stood right in front of the proprietor, who circumvented him, still refusing to acknowledge his presence. As he walked off, the young man said:

"It's my father, isn't it? He's dying, isn't he?"

The proprietor said nothing. This was a hateful, evil, painful silence.

Then the ice melted. But his answer made no sense to me, and it hurt the boy.

"He's not your father."

The young man said nothing. He rushed to the door, suddenly full of purpose, but couldn't get it to open.

The proprietor said, "I hope you aren't thinking of going home. Your aunt's son is at the door waiting for you, and he's ready to kill you."

The boy paused to think. He had lost all resolve. His face dissolved in confusion. Driving himself through the wind that was trying to hurl him back inside, he left.

For a time, I kept my questions to myself. The proprietor had his back to me. He was making a lot of noise washing something. I waited for him to finish. But whatever he was doing, he was taking his time. At last he turned around.

"For God's sake, tell me what's going on!" I cried.

As he removed his apron, the proprietor seemed to search for words.

The door opened. Another young man came back in, an old man at his side.

"I gave him his blessing. Has the other one slipped away yet?"

The proprietor's hands were behind his back, clutching the ties of his apron. Instead of untying them, he did them up again. He came over to my table. It was as if he thought I needed to hear what he had to say.

"Kamil Ağa, the driver, he's just died. That dog you saw over there by the stove, that was his son. But he took his sister down the wrong path. His father cast him out."

Then he turned to the other men.

"He has no honor. He says so himself. But not out of remorse. He came back hoping for his inheritance."

One of the old men arranged his face to show that he was impartial.

"Even if he showed remorse," he said, "there would be no forgiveness."

I have no idea why I asked the question that now came to my lips. Why I didn't pause to consider what effect my foolish words might have.

"What happened to the girl?" I asked.

Then something strange happened. Without so much as lifting their eyes, these men exchanged glances. No one spoke as we sank into a very different sort of silence.

Without lifting their eyes, they challenged the silence, and its stillness.

"Why did you ask?"

"What was the point?"

"Was that the only thing you could think to ask?"

"Why are you so curious all of a sudden?"

The one who asked this last question took a menacing tone.

No one offered me an answer. I left my money on the table. I glanced over at the proprietor. He was still lost in thought, head bowed. His skin was yellow. He was still trying to untie his apron. I opened the door and stepped outside. I had not been able to find out what happened to the girl, so why was I so sure that this coffeehouse owner had rescued her from the wrong path?

I Just Don't Know Why I Keep Doing These Things

. . .

In the evenings I go out to a rather ordinary coffeehouse on a crowded avenue. I go straight to a table right behind the ones next to the window, and for the next few hours, I just sit there, watching the people passing by. Do I ever get bored? On the contrary, I enjoy it tremendously. Do I examine people's faces and observe their behavior and think up stories about them? Chance would be a fine thing. How could that be anyone's idea of a good time? So how do I amuse myself? I think about dying, and I think about growing old; I think about all the wars that haven't happened yet . . . The darker the thoughts I let into my mind, the better I amuse myself.

Everyone on this earth is evil. Life has no meaning. Only an idiot would fall in love . . . And so on, and so on. So all right. You're asking how it could be any fun to entertain such thoughts. If you want to know, then just think about it. What you do is find the easy way out. Here's the hardest one: the remedy for death! I convince myself I'm not going to die, and then I'm fine. Go on, give it a try.

What this means is that after you've mastered all your grimmest thoughts, you gain entrance to a new world where everyone is laughing, and everyone is content. It's only at the very beginning that you feel glum. After that, there's no problem. You're back to being the man you were. You're happy without a care in the world. . . . Or not! At the end of this journey from bad to good, I leave the coffeehouse, and there I am again, walking the streets, thinking about death, and wars, and rising prices, and worries about the future – but never mind!

Just as I'm leaving the coffeehouse, this old man walks in. He's all bones. How tiresome to have to go through the motions of shaving every day, isn't there a better way? It's always the same two-day beard. How does he keep it from growing, why is it always exactly the same? Now that's something to admire.

His eyes are the same black as the black on his grizzled cheeks. His eyelashes, too: what power I see there. The place on the map of Turkey where I put his birthplace: Van. Whether it's true or not – that doesn't concern me, not one bit. If he turned out to be from Istanbul, or Balıkesir, I'd still say the same thing: "You're wrong, old man. You've forgotten. You can't be from Balıkesir, you're from Van. So stop lying! What's wrong with Van? Don't you like it there? If only you could see Lake Van as I see it, when I close my eyes . . . It's surrounded by snow-capped mountains. Go down to the water's edge at night and you'll see wild men on winged horses skirting the lake's silent shores. And pale, whiter than white, black-eyed girls washing their clothes in the water. Everything is like that water. Nothing's fit to drink. You have to see it with your own eyes to get any sense of it. And the wind – I don't know what they call it, but even at the dead of night it sends little ripples to the shore, and the whole surface shimmers. When the gulls of Lake Van call out, women give birth to sons, and fillies colts, and cows calves. Only when the waters of the lake are still can a person die. You're telling a lie, old man. You're from Van. I can tell just from your prayer beads. Yes, I can tell just from those amber prayer beads you're slapping against the palm of your hand. Why do you keep insisting you're from Balıkesir? You're from Van, you hear? You're from Van!"

He would go to the table next to the window, take out his silver-rimmed glasses and settle down to read the paper. When I said this happened just as I was leaving, I was telling the truth. But I still had the chance to see him place his melon-colored velvet eyeglass case on the table, and put on his glasses to read the paper. Because after I took my leave of the coffee-house, I would stroll past the window four or five more times, as part of my evening promenade.

He was somewhere between fifty and eighty years of age. If he'd told you he was fifty, you'd tell yourself he looked pretty rough and had aged before his time. If he'd said he was eighty, you'd have nothing to say except, "Maşallah! You look so much younger!" Who is he, what is he, when did he arrive here from Van, what sort of work does he do? I'm afraid I can't answer these questions. But there's no doubt he's a bachelor. He must be renting a room in some cheap hotel. He must be doing the sort of little job that people from Van do in this city. I was never able to pin down what he did exactly. A middleman, I thought. A tradesman. A head porter. A retired porter. A nightwatchman. I tried out all these ideas, but none of them quite fit. In the end, though, I found a job for him. When I looked at him closely, I noticed that his suit came from a good tailor. Yes, I thought. He must be a retired law clerk.

When I saw him sitting there, his free hand propped on the table and his amber prayer beads dangling from the side of his chair, I would try to imagine what he was reading.

And so it went on. It surprised me how he always managed to arrive at exactly the same moment I was leaving, and before long it began to get on my nerves. In the end I got into the habit of preparing to leave before he even came through the door. I'd watch him come in and sit down and put on his glasses, and then I'd leave.

One night, I had some business. I got to the coffeehouse later than usual. The old man was already seated at his table. I took the table just behind him. It was already late. The coffeehouse was almost empty. The old man had long since finished his paper, and now he was gazing at the street outside.

And so I did the same. When he lit a cigarette, I lit one, too. Then he took out those prayer beads, those amber prayer beads he always brought with him. He began to pass them through his fingers. Click, click, click. If I'd had a set of my own, I'd have done the same. But I had no prayer beads, so I couldn't. And that really annoyed me. He was looking out at the street, and I was looking at him, and he looked sad. But it was not the sort of sadness that comes with death, or heartbreak. I began to wonder what sort of thing it might come from. I thought: money worries. And as we'll soon see, I turned out to be right. Who knows what effect money worries might have on a person's face, or manner, or complexion? Maybe I didn't know, maybe it was a coincidence. Somehow I divined the fact that this man was suffering from money worries, without his telling me. For a while I put the old man out of my mind and just looked out at the street. If I said that I didn't even notice when he rose from the table to vanish like a ghost, I wouldn't be lying.

The next day, when I arrived at the coffeehouse at the normal time, I saw that something strange had happened. The old man had arrived two and a half hours before schedule. Once again, I took the table right behind him. Suddenly he turned with a smile to look me straight in the eyes.

"Yesterday evening," he said. "I hung my prayer beads right there, on my chair . . . and now I've lost them."

So much emotion on his face: he was bursting with hope, and with worry. He was agitated. His usually sallow skin had gone pale. That five-millimeter beard of his was quivering.

"I'm so sorry," I said. "What a terrible shame."

"Only yesterday, I took them to the Bedesten to sell them. They offered seventy but I wouldn't take it. I wanted eighty. If only I'd taken their money," he said.

"They were valuable then, I take it?"

"Of course. They were amber. The purest kind, too: Balgami!"

"I'm sure you're right. They were very handsome indeed."

"You probably saw me holding them last night."

"To tell you the truth, I wasn't paying attention."

All at once, his expression changed. Suddenly I was the enemy. I could see the hatred burning in his eyes.

"I'm going to the police," he said.

"You should," I said.

For a moment, I thought he was going to say: "You took them. I know full well. Hand them over." He even looked as if he were going to say it. I kept my cool.

Again his expression changed.

"If I ever find the man who took it, believe you me . . ."

"It won't be easy!" I said.

Without raising his eyes, he bit his lip.

. . .

Day after day, he came to the coffeehouse early. He never greeted me, but as he took his usual seat, he'd make it clear he'd seen me. Without so much as a glance in my direction, he would read his paper, and everything about him – his pallor, his fury – told me that he was sure I'd stolen his prayer beads. When I got up to leave, he would follow me with his eyes, as I caught him doing a few times when I pretended to have forgotten my cigarettes on the table and went back to get them.

The other night we were seated at our usual places. He was reading his paper, and I was scribbling down a few thoughts. Then, suddenly, I looked up. The coffeehouse has mirrors running along its walls, and I was looking into one of them. This man wasn't looking at me, this I could see, but I could also see why from his vantage point he would be driven to accuse me – and stranger still, when I looked at the way I was sitting, I could see something in me of the brazen thief who could pull off this sort of thing and still keep his cool. So I took a close look at myself. Yes, I did look as if I'd stolen his prayer beads. You know how children will sometimes insist they didn't do something bad. And they really haven't. But there's something in their face that says they did. It's because they haven't done it that they can't look natural. So that's what I was like. Like one of those children.

Things remain very strange between me and the old man. Last night, a friend came by my house and left behind a set of prayer beads made out of seashells. I passed in front of the coffeehouse holding them in my hand. I didn't really notice what was going on inside. I was heading to the tram stop just a little further on. Then, suddenly, the old man was there next to me. In the dark he must not have been able to see my prayer beads clearly. From the corner of my eye, I could see him staring at those prayer beads. I didn't even have to turn in his direction. I just kept clicking those seashells. If you saw how furious he was as he walked off. Just the way he turned his humpback on me, I could hear what he was thinking: "And now you're taunting me! You have no shame!"

The worst of it is that I hardly ever go to that coffeehouse now, and if he's there sitting at the window when I do, I act as if I have something hidden in my pocket when I pass by. Sometimes I have to struggle to keep myself from smiling. Or I whistle. And even if I don't, I still feel like I'm hiding something in my pocket. And I see him thinking that maybe he should just go to the police and tell them. But then he'll kill the thought. "You son of a dog! He's doing that on purpose! Would he do that if he had any prayer beads in his pocket? And I'm sure that bum has long since pawned it off. May you see the benefits!" I'm the worst kind of man. I'm a thief, without stealing a thing.

I feel bad for that poor old man, too. I even go so far as to look into his eyes, as if to say I've stolen his prayer beads and feel no remorse. That's a terrible thing to do, I know. I know it, but I can't help myself. He's the one who makes me feel like this. You'd think that after doing all this I might feel just a little guilty, but no! What if I told you that sometimes when I pass that coffeehouse, I look all around me, sometimes surreptitiously, sometimes very openly, moving my head from side to side – and I laugh, in a way that would make anyone who saw me wonder if I was crazy or who knows what else? If I told you that, what would you say?

Milk

. . .

I did something just now that I haven't done in years: I drank milk. The steam in that shop, the smell of milk – it took me back across four decades – returned me to my cradle, reducing me to tears and lulling me to sleep. Yes, it's the truth I'm telling you. It had been years since I'd got up early and years since I'd last drunk milk. There was a time when I started each new day with milk. How greedily we all clung to our mother's breasts back then. How monstrous those toothless gums on her nipples. How sad that we have no memories of our mothers' milk or our first sight of the world, through eyes made blurry by the tears we shed for milk . . .

We begin our days with milk and we finish them with wine, but this morning, from the moment that first cry rose up in me, from that first pang of hunger, I knew those days were over. Over and done with. The moment I walked through the door of the dairy shop, my old life abandoned me. And this is what I said to the flotsam that tried to come in after me: my first cry, my cradle, my mother's milk, my loves and hates, my public face, my private life, my days of wine, and *rakı*, and cards, and women, and lust, and my many fine days in the company of friends. This is what I said to the child who was crying for milk – the child I never knew, and would never learn to know:

"So we're leaving you here, outside. You say you wanted to drink milk? Nonsense! We've had our fill of milk! What sort of man are you anyway? Shame on you. This is the last straw. This is where we part. You've sunk so low as to bring me to this shop. It's all over between us . . ."

Turning around, I cried:

"Get lost!" And off they went, toppling over each other in the wind.

I walked into the shop like a man reborn. And how I longed to shout out the good news. I was beginning a new life! From now on I would wake up fresh as a newborn to the fragrance of hot and foaming milk, and its white mist would fill my nostrils until at last I sneezed. The milk I had taken from my mother's breasts would come out through my nose. I would have my breakfast at a dairy shop that was foaming with the fragrance of milk. My new life would begin here. I would ascend to a world steeped in the scent of milk. After forty-two years of burning my nostrils with hot olive oil I would be delivered to this faraway land of peace and freedom, this land of milk, to begin anew.

My hands are cracked, my skin as dark as earth. I'm proud and I'm free, because at long last I have vanquished the monster in the cradle, and to mark this glorious day I shall drink in the milk foaming in my bowl like a man whose beard has gone white.

Outside it's raining. But I am still inside. I'd seen off my past, and I was feeling fine. I don't miss my old life, not one little bit. One bowl of milk and I've sent it packing. I've lifted up the mansion of the past. I've closed my eyes to the memories flashing from each window, and smashed it to bits.

And still it rains. Let it rain, what do I care? Let it rain forever. A line of poetry floats into my mind:

"We never knew the spring day when we were weaned . . ."

And that was when I knew I had to free myself of all the verse, couplets, novels and books. I was entering a new world. I required poems just as new. I needed to start reading new novels, viewing new paintings, and to write I needed to forge a new Turkish. I needed to seek out new sentiments, new books, new ideas. But what of the flotsam I'd left at the dairy shop's iron door? What if they mobbed me when I left? What if they herded me back to my old bad habits? The chain that binds the milk of memory with the future – it forms a ring, doesn't it? It's bound unto itself. When I was back on the rainy street, when I had rounded up my runaways, here's what I'd say to them: "What a fool I was back there in that dairy shop. Why didn't you warn me? Please forgive me. Everyone gets like that sometimes. I hope you're not offended by me. Forgive me, please."

"Would you like another serving?" asked the man in the dairy shop. I drank one more cup. No, it no longer had the same effect.

The everyday world waiting outside in the rain said this to me: "Come on, now. Hurry. Enough is enough. Come out here. You need to be with us. You can't spend the whole day in the dairy shop, pretending you're a newborn. We're out here waiting. We're coming to get you. Everything and everyone is out here waiting. Time to finish this game you've been playing with them inside. No one's ever born again. And even if you could be. What would happen then? In two years, no, not even two years, in two days we'd turn you back into the old you. The old you who thinks only of himself, with the same jealousies, the same ill humor, the old you who drinks too much and is a fool. We have all we need to knock you out with the old maladies. And what sort of new world did you have in mind, my dear man? A world never seen, or heard, or tasted, or written . . . are you serious? Come on now. Come back to the life you know. No milk for you tonight. Tonight you're going to drink pure molasses mixed with water and grain alcohol. And then you'll feel good, and your old hopes will come crowding back –

the fond wishes that the hand cannot grasp and the eye cannot see and can only rarely be so much as felt, and the half-baked illusions that are clear to the naked eye, and begin with wine, and overflow with drunken heroics . . . When you greet these old friends again, you will be ashamed of the state you were in this morning.

"Tomorrow morning when we wake you up, you'll have a foul, fusty, pasty mouth, like you always do."

By now the aroma of foaming milk was streaming down the walls of the dairy shop. I put on my hat. I raced out into the street. Hearing my shouts – "Stay away from me! Stay away!" – my runaways approached me softly, warily, the way doctors or nurses or guards might round in on a mental patient in distress. They took my arm. They stroked my shoulder, and then, in one fell swoop, they all grabbed my collar. And suddenly, I found myself all buttoned up inside my crazy shirt, and back in my old crazy life.

Two glasses of milk. Oh, look what you've done to me.

Fire Tongs and a Chair
on a Winter's Night

. . .

It's getting on my nerves, this empty room. And that clock on the wall, tick, tick, and tocking, while the chair just sits there. The snow is coming down faster than before. It turns me to ice just to look at it. I feel like I need to do something. But I know I can't do a thing. I could jump on a ferry and head for the city. Take my chances. It's always there waiting for me: that street lottery with its hopes and its perils, its noise and its twists of fate. I plunge my hand into the game bag and pull out my numbers: 77 red! 19, *tombola!*

Precisely nine miles between me and the city. Water surrounding me, on all four sides. The snow slows down, and then picks up again. A rooster starts crowing. A child chasing a turkey. I hear the tolling of a bell and in the distance a phaeton. Again, the rooster crows.

That empty chair needs filling. But who would ever sit here? There's nobody I want to see. That chair, though . . . doesn't it look like it's expecting someone? The carpenter who made it, he had a head on his shoulders. He knew this chair was destined to sit here like this, waiting for people.

I peel an orange and eat it.

I must have dozed off, because the clock stopped ticking. But now it's back at it. The snow is coming down slower again. The tongs on the wood-burning stove remind me of the chair. Someone should take them and pull out an ember, blow off the ash, and hold it out for me to light my cigarette.

I can just see that gypsy woman selling tongs along the shacks on the hills of Mecidiyeköy. Now she's waving the very same tongs and shouting at her husband:

"Hey old man! These tongs are different! It's like they're calling out for fire just for the fun of it!"

"What the hell, Kehlibar. You lost your marbles? Come on, Kehlibar! Stop talking nonsense."

"But I'm telling you, old man. These tongs are looking for my fire!"

Her husband has gray flecks in his moustache, more black than white. He looks around forty-five. His teasing eyes are shot with blood; they speak to me of fear.

As if to say, "Never you mind. The wife's got a screw loose."

But like me, the gypsy woman likes the way the tongs just sit there. And not only the way the tongs just sit there: the way they conjure up a helping hand, a dear friend, and an evening of good stories. She can see it all. Kehlibar is a lonely, troubled, and mysterious woman; she lives in her imagination. Her husband is jealous beyond belief. He sends her out with the other women, to sell tongs with the other women, and he's on pins and needles until she gets home.

I light my cigarette. I face the window, to watch the heavy snowflakes falling. And suddenly I am shrouded by bliss. Where did it come from? I just don't know. How did it arise from such a dark mood? It fits me as snugly as a shoe on a beautiful little lady's soft foot. But what can I make of it?

I draw back the curtains. And I am a child again, thinking about my new rubber boots with their red lining, wondering if they'll squeak in the snow on my way to school in the morning. Where to hang this happy moment? There beside two cloves of garlic and the evil eye? Later we tossed bird feed, millet, corn, and wheat under a cherry tree; we came out from the house with a sieve; we tied a pole to the edge of the sieve so we could lift it up; we tied a string to the pole; we threw the string down to a blue-eyed boy looking up from a lower window in the house, and he tied the end of the string to a stone and went back inside to munch on the hot orange peels drying on the wood-burning stove while he waited by the window for sparrows to fly into the trap . . .

Oh that miserable, foolish childhood of mine! Even you are gone. Your voice is so soft that it could be coming to me from the grave.

The wind jumps from roof to roof, slipping over the lead domes. A shadow takes shape in the sky. Growing in the mist on the windowpane, the shadow is now a crow. Now it is perched on top of the church across the street. Now why did it have to go and land right on top of the holy cross?

The north wind is blowing like mad. The old banks of snow look like corpses, bruised and purple, but the hailstones pelting down on them look like millet, glowing gold.

I might leave the house, I might go to a coffeehouse; I might think about whether or not I should go to Istanbul. I might miss the boat back and when night has fallen over the city I might stagger home on a cane. I might sit and read. I might read love stories. We might assume that human love starts here. We might close our minds to our lives, and life itself, and think only of ourselves. We might never stick our heads outside. We might drive away all thoughts of hunger and sickness and people without heating or fire or wood-burning stoves; we might lose ourselves in love stories as we unravel into dreams.

Let the fire tongs and the chair just sit there and wait. Bastards! The birds will always fly up into the sky to look down with piercing eyes. Let's see if they can spy one tiny piece, one tiny grain of millet.

The snow is falling. Some people come home dressed in fur, some in fancy boots, some in rubber shoes, some in spiked boots, and some holding a cane.

Winter is a nasty business! An evil thing, evil! Turn your eyes away from all the pomp! Turn your eyes from this fake Swiss landscape . . .

I stand up and push the ever-waiting chair under the table. And those sad fire tongs, still waiting for a human hand – I pull them out from the embers. I lay them beside the stove. The wind and snow have stopped. A cloak of silence has fallen over the village. The sky is pitch black. This vast and neverending winter night is still, is at rest, but once again gathering up more snow. I open first the window and then my mouth to curse the winter night with a foul curse I learned long ago from an Armenian fisherman in Kumkapı.

A Story about Springtime

. . .

A holiday, an awakening, a miracle, a folly. It's never going to come, and then it does. Springtime answers to all these descriptions, and many others, too . . . Birds and butterflies, poppies and meadows, green grass and blossoms, mimosas and oleanders, dandelions and the sound of water, gypsies and lambs . . . You can find them all in a classic springtime, and there's even room for the tendril of a vine. Of all the memories I've lost, the most important is the sunlight in April and May.

Of all the seasons, spring is the one that a man over forty cannot face without some sadness. Where has she gone, that girl whose hands went suddenly pale? That wind that turned her pale? That fast-beating heart? They're right, the ones who divide life itself into seasons. We each have our spring, our summer, our autumn and winter. For us, spring comes much later than it does for animals. A horse has its springtime when it's one. Well, all right, maybe two. A lamb can become a ram at six months. But a child can't really understand springtime before the age of twenty. Any taste of it before then is a false spring. That's the sort of story I'm writing here: it's about one of those false springs.

Exactly thirty years ago, I was twelve years old and living in an Anatolian city. My father was a civil servant. We'd arrived in this city in late summer. We'd struggled through a bad winter – snowdrifts as high as a man. Then one day, spring came. The snow melted. The snow melted, but it wasn't the sun's doing. It was the rain's. In Anatolian cities, spring begins with an afternoon deluge. In the mornings the sky is a bright blue, and the sun looks as cold as if it's sparkling on snow. Toward eleven, a black cloud rolls in – it could be from the east, or the west, or the north. Ten minutes later, it begins to pour – pour like water from a glass. And that's it, for the rest of the day. Great lashes of rain, one after the other. Through my window I could see a dark green pasture, known in the vicinity as "Black Meadow." I would never have felt the urge to burst out of the house screaming like a madman if not for that play of colors on the meadow that, like the sea, soaked up every pigment of the sky.

I had been in poor health all winter. Every time I went out into the cold, my head would spin. Then there was this strange, oppressive stretch of rain and black clouds, with three gloomy days for every bright one, but there was also spring, filling the air with the aroma of earth and meadow, people and barns, and all I wanted to do was shout and cry and then lie still.

One morning I was gazing at the ceiling. The clouds hadn't rolled in yet. The sky was still sparkling. I lay on my mattress, wondering how long it would be before the rain came. Just then a bright bird flew through my room. I sat up in bed. It flew past again. Then, on the wall to my right, I saw a band of light flicker and disappear. Then it vanished. I rubbed my eyes. When I looked again I could see a bright circle, shaking and trembling. It seemed to be trying to pin itself to the wall. This was light reflecting off a mirror – it could be nothing else.

I jumped out of bed to look out the window. Our upper garden looked out onto the garden of the house beneath us. The light on my wall must have come from a mirror somewhere over there. She was sitting on a wicker mat among the peach blossoms. Behind her she had placed a chair. She must have been sixteen or seventeen. I did not leave the window. When the light from her mirror touched my eyes, I didn't shield them with my hands. I looked straight in front of me, eyes unblinking.

The next day I, too, had a mirror in my hands. When the light from my mirror hit her eyes, she'd avert them, smiling faintly. This game never lasted longer than half an hour. She would race back into her house with rain dripping from her hair, and I would return to my bed. The next day would bring another beautiful morning, and it would always be her mirror that arrived first, racing across my room to hover trembling on the wall, as if looking for a hook to hang from. And again I would look straight into her mirror light, my eyes unblinking; as she shielded her beautiful eyes, we would together gaze at mine. Then the clouds would roll in, with the afternoon deluge. Nothing else interested me, and that is why I paid no attention to the horse carriage that stopped outside our house one morning. Only my mother caught me playing with my mirror. She had an odd expression on her face as she took in the garden, the girl, the light from the mirror, and the mirror in my hands.

"Come on now," she said. "Get dressed."

We got into the carriage. Behind us, they'd tied on two trunks to carry our belongings. My father had a new posting. Off we went. As we passed through a forest, the sun came bursting through the clouds, lighting up the new leaves on the trees, and then disappeared. And, with a pang, I remembered the mirror light that I would never see again. I burst into tears. My father asked:

"What's wrong with this one?"

I buried my head in my mother's scarf. I have no idea what she conveyed to my father, if not with her hands, then with her eyes, but neither said a thing. Somehow knowing that no one had the courage to stop me, I cried my heart out.

And now, whenever a light happens to pass across my window in the springtime, I remember that day with the sweet sadness we all share at that time of year, with a restless beating heart. Thirty years have passed since that day. Never once have I flashed a mirror in anyone's face, and never once has anyone flashed a mirror into mine. But if a light happened to pass through my room on a spring day, as fast as a swallow, I don't know what would become of me.

Sinağrit Baba

. . .

We were five rowboats at Hell's Point. A beautiful January evening. A southern wind. Splashes of red rippling over the sea. Long, vast, dying waves the color of strong linden tea. The boats rocking heavily in the sea, fishing poles in suspense, silent souls . . .

Does a creature lurk beneath us, woven from the darkest of the seven colors, drifting through the hushed and twisted caverns thirty-eight fathoms deep? How can it be, that Sinağrit Baba has left the hunt so soon? He's the king of the deeps, lavishing kindness and magnificence on all he leaves in his wake. His jacket, noble but cruel with its shimmering rainbow scales. He is rushing back to his palace; it's made of gold, emerald, coral, and mother-of-pearl, all twinkling in the dark blue.

Sinağrit Baba hasn't said a word in his life, he's never married and he's always lived alone. How many tragedies has he watched from his cavern's emerald window? How many fishing lines has he dragged into the sea?

But tonight he will choose a line and put an end to his long life. He will end his long life while every scale on his jacket is still sparkling, and long before mayonnaise is smeared over his flesh. Though there is still time before he is devoured by that pale and sticky creature, the wretched stingray, he knows he should surrender now to that intelligent creature from the strange world above, to be feted at a sumptuous feast served with white wine.

Sinağrit Baba sniffs one of the lines. It belongs to the fisherman Hristo. He's a flawed man. Greedy and always calculating. Yes, he's poor, but he's not proud. Sinağrit Baba favors poor men with some pride. He drifts to the next line and sniffs. Hasan's line. Forget him. Forget his temper, too. Underneath it, he's a coward, and Sinağrit Baba favors the brave. He tries another line. Fisherman Yakup is a good man about town, charming, loveable, and sometimes crude. But he has a jealous streak. Sinağrit Baba doesn't favor jealous men. Forget him, too. The next line belongs to a stingy man. Whereas Sinağrit Baba favors generosity. Nevertheless he tries the bait and, tearing off half a Spanish mackerel, he flattens the hook entirely and swallows the bait whole before its stingy owner yanks up his line.

"Holy mother, Nikoli," he says. "He's completely flattened the hook."

With Nikoli's bait in his belly, Sinağrit Baba tries to find a flaw in Nikoli. Surely he's flawed. First of all, he's a drunk. And he's immoral and self-centered. But he's also generous and brave. He's hardly a coward. He's poor. He's proud. Sinağrit Baba favors the poor and the proud, but not Nikoli's brand of pride. Sinağrit is after something just a bit different: a pride that's timely and true; but no, that's not quite it either, it's something you sense in the way a fisherman holds his rod, something about him that goes down to the very roots of his hair, the best of humankind. Sinağrit Baba can't flatten a fishhook borne by a proud hand, or sever his line, or make away with his barrel swivel.

He sniffs all five of the rowboats, and he isn't pleased.

Sinağrit Baba hovers beside the corner of his cavern, watching the sea palace sparkle, lit by the mercury bait and the hooks shimmering soft as moonlight in the deep blue sea. More lines drop down and soon fifteen mercury lamps are swinging softly in the center of the land of Sinağrit and Çüpra . . . One after the other red bream dart out from their hollows and attack the lamps, foolishly snagging themselves on the hooks. Pulled up to the surface, their eyes wide as they turn and look down, unsure if they should give in and see the world above them or struggle back down into theirs. Their eyes grow wider still as they look down at Sinağrit Baba, as if to say, "save us from this horrible fate." Sinağrit Baba takes a moment's pause. He only has to swim over to the shimmering line and bite through it, nothing more. But he stays still and decides not to save them. He knows it would be an easy thing to do, but he knows something else, too: that reason can't fix these things, that it makes no difference if you are animal, vegetable or human being, if you live in the water, on land or in the air. His good deed would only have a real and lasting effect when all the other fish in the sea understand that severing the shimmering line meant saving all the others. The Mighty Sinağrit might bite through the line, but then who would save him when his own time came? Who would ever think of biting the line for him?

A brightly shimmering hook falls into the sea. Hopeful, the Mighty Sinağrit swims toward it and sniffs. The owner's vaguely familiar. Nibbling a little on the bait, he thinks for a moment that this is the very man he is looking for. Then suddenly he's caught. Tumbling into the boat, the Mighty Sinağrit stares up at the fisherman with wide and joyful eyes. Again and again, he looks up through his luminous, red-rimmed black eyes. Then he flaps his body up and down on the bottom of the boat like a furious young girl pounding her foot on the floor. Maybe he sees something in the man we can't see: that this man has failed the test. Yes, he has led a brave and generous life. And he lives as a proud man, something the Mighty Sinağrit thinks is good. But somehow now he knows that this man is a wretched dog; he sees what no one else can see. This man who just fished him out of the sea has never put his courage, his bravery, his pride to the test over the years; he's been that lucky. But who is he? What is he? Sinağrit Baba doesn't know. But he's understood that, despite having lived a generous, proud, and courageous life, this man has failed the test. And might never have been tested at all, he might end his days like that. Sinağrit Baba has never encountered anything like it. Just before he dies, he looks up at the man again. From his forehead alone, he knows the man to be the most dishonorable of all dishonorable men, the most cowardly of all cowards. But he will die a brave and honorable and generous man. He has been so fortunate throughout life that he never once considered his duplicity. Would Sinağrit Baba have surrendered willingly to him if he had? So he flails desperately about in the boat again, his mouth fixed in a silent scream. Then it closes. It was with regret and a swell of defeat that the Mighty Sinağrit gives his dying breath in that rowboat, watching humanity fail the test.

Four Plusses

. . .

You want to light up but you don't have a match. Where will you go for a light? You need directions. Who to ask? You see a crowd gathering. You wonder what's going on. Who will you turn to? A man like me. And while I do like being the one people are more likely to turn to when they've lost their way, or need a match, there are times when I don't. But I can't say I have never assumed an arrogant air to discourage the poor souls who walk over to me with a question, or who look at me as if they might spring one on me . . . but who knows, I was so very low that day. So many times I've had to ask myself why I've acted that way when I usually disliked being the one picked out of the crowd. It also annoys me when young boys ask me to light their cigarettes. They stand there, some distance away, sizing me up. And then the strange way they come up to me. There have been times when I've let them down. And it was on those occasions that I came to understand what a terrible thing it is, to be wrong about someone. There is not a soul on earth who can bear it. I've seen quite a few of them give up on the idea of asking me for a light. Some people make sure never to risk losing hope.

I myself can recall a number of times when I have faltered while trying to find the right person to ask for directions. After which I lost patience and went straight over to the man closest to me. Some didn't show me the way even if they knew, while others were so delighted to have the chance to offer me a cigarette that they couldn't stop smiling. How wonderful it is, not to know how to thank a man who has shown fellowship at the moment you least expected it; first you say, *merci beaucoup*, then, thanks so much, then, I can't thank you enough; then you translate the French: you explain to the man that it means "thank you very much."

But I know this, too: if a stranger asks you a question, if he's picked you out of twenty people, he's already made a number of calculations. These are calculations of a psychological nature.

And then, if he's mixed in some hollow, inscrutable theories about physiognomy . . . This reminds me of the professor who did all that research on the science of the face. How carefully he studied his faces. And what outlandish things the poor doctor read into them. Oh, that intense gaze, that wrinkled face, those evenly aligned strands of dark hair that framed the beauty of a face. But he got them all wrong. There was nothing in that wise and intense gaze, bar stupidity, nothing in that lined face but the idiotic fancies of a young girl. Beneath that broad forehead framed by that mane of black hair, there was nothing but lost memories of an empty life.

Most of us cannot make heads or tails of psychology or face-reading; rather, we proceed as amateurs, knowing nothing about these sciences, lighting our cigarettes, inquiring after ferries, asking for directions, or whatever else we need to know. Our habits take over – we lose all sense of shame. So why is it that they'll pick me out of a crowd of young men? Is it because yours truly is a good man? I doubt it . . . They don't choose me because I'm a good person. They choose me because I seem to be just the right man to ask. Does that mean I have a compelling face? What a fine thing that would be! There must be another reason. Are we shabbily dressed? Are our boots unpolished? Did they catch a foolish glint in our eyes? Forbearance in our manner? A kink in our nose? Something slack about our cheeks? Or is the knot in our tie a touch too shiny? It has to be something. It could just be that I have something of the vagabond in me. If you saw a man jumping out of a car and dashing for the ferry – would you even think of asking him a question? If you saw a gentleman frowning as he drew deeply from his cigarette outside a restaurant he had evidently just left, would you even think of asking him for a light? If you saw a traveler dripping with elegance, would you ask him directions? Could you ever find the courage to approach a man wearing polished boots, to ask him why the crowd?

Things being as they are, I rarely get angry when people ask me for directions, or if they come to me for a light. And when I am coming to see you, my love, and someone asks for directions, I even take the time to have my boots shined.

I hate it, though, when an immaculately dressed city type asks me for a light. If you want to know why, it's because he couldn't find the courage to ask all those other men, and so this man . . . Though when you think about it, this has nothing to do with courage. He was embarrassed by all those others, but not by me. Truth is, this sort of thing annoys me. Because even if it isn't rude, it's a bit strange. You can't ask just anyone. Why am I the one they choose? Here's my answer: I like it when a villager asks for directions without thinking about it first, or making any calculations – without knowing the first thing about psychology or physiognomy. Let them come to me with their questions. They aren't seething with secret thoughts or clever schemes. And how could these poor creatures ever dare approach that fat man oozing with pride, his every pore scrubbed clean? I'm just someone who happens to be there – a man like any other.

My love! I shouldn't prattle on like this, when I have a story to tell. But what am I to do? Am I not to look for a man to light my cigarette with his if I have no matches? Do you expect me to give up smoking? I can't even give up writing these damn stories. I just sit there, idling, cigarette in hand, as if looking for someone. Hemmed in by so many important, conceited, grave-faced men, I hardly know where to begin.

Listen. This just occurred to me. It's good to be asked for a light. It's neither good nor bad to be asked for directions, or to look like the right person to be asked. It's strange, isn't it? If you look around you, my love, you'll see that – male or female – we all have our excesses. One person might be overly arrogant, and another overly jealous; for every overdressed person, there is another who is dressed in rags; for every smart aleck there is a snob. This one over here is too dirty, and that one over there is too clean. There's no middle ground, my dearest. And neither do I wish to choose, or be chosen. It's probably best just to vote! There's a sin in that, too. It's best, my friend, to carry matches and know where you're going, and never go out without knowing which way you are going. What right do we have, my love, to prejudge every man we meet?

Time for my story. I was waiting for the ferry. No, I wasn't actually waiting for the ferry. I was waiting to miss the ferry home. I said that wrong. I was waiting to miss the ferry so as not to go home. The very thought of going back to my silent, empty village – it was more than I could bear. Better to stay in Istanbul, drinking away the hours, and thinking of you . . . But sadly the ferry was still waiting at the pier. I stayed in my seat. I stayed in my seat, waiting for it to leave. At last it pulled away. And I relaxed. I lit a cigarette. I had a match.

Sitting just across from me, there was a youngish man, in his hand a piece of paper. He kept looking at it. The passenger lounge emptied, and then it filled up again. At last the man looked up from the paper in his hand.

He looked around. I could see what he was after. He had no idea what it said on this piece of paper. Someone had to explain it to him.

I moved my eyes away from him. I fixed them on something else. On the eyes of a woman who wasn't looking at me. And this was when it began to get on my nerves, knowing that of all the people in this lounge and for reasons I would never understand, I would be the one he chose. And for a moment I considered why he probably chose me – I was an important man who could understand what was written on this piece of paper. And why would I lie? As soon as this idea came to me – no, I didn't decide I was an important person, but what if I said that the idea of being chosen suddenly appealed to me? I threw a quick glance in his direction. Though by then he'd already chosen me. And here, if you like, you can imagine that I've said that to win your favor . . .

The man came over to me. He held out the piece of paper.

"For the love of God" he said. "Could you take a look at this for me?"

I looked, but I couldn't quite understand it. I read through it again, and then again. I felt a pain in my heart. The same pain you feel in the summer, if you're very thirsty, and you've gulped down a glass of cold water too fast – a heaviness, that's what I felt inside me. I looked up at the man.

"I'm just on my way to work," he said. "I've found a very good job. If only you knew, sir, how long I've gone without work. But now I've found a job. I'm engaged, too. They examined me, and I'm in perfect health. At the very end, they did a blood test. They say they had to. How is my blood – is it as good as the rest of me?"

He was smiling, but on his forehead I could see the shadow of a doubt. I remembered the professor. And I wondered if I too had turned into a physiognomist. No. Here was someone who had, at long last, found a job. He was holding a piece of paper, and it was covered with suspicious marks . . . No! This was a man whose worries had found their way into his eyes and the middle of his forehead. He had been given three blood tests. And each time the result had four plusses: ++++.*

"Have you been ill at all, my friend?"

"No, not at all," he said.

His face went taut. His eyes drained of color.

"I really don't know much about these things. I can't really understand it," I said.

"There's nothing wrong. Do you think?"

"Probably not," I said. "I'm not a doctor. I can't really make sense of it."

"Should I take this paper with me?" he asked. "I mean, to the office where I'll be working?"

I said nothing. I examined his face carefully. My gaze was not so much careful as needlessly – stupidly – pitying . . .

I had that pitying look from you, once . . . I asked you how to get some-where: how to find happiness, to be precise. Do you remember?

What my eyes said to that man, I cannot know . . . Once again we examined the paper. I didn't tell him to take it into his new job with him, but neither did I tell him not to. He wants to look, and I am looking into his eyes. The man's gone deathly pale.

I left. I had my shoes shined. I ran home. I shaved. I put on a new tie. I assumed an arrogant air, so that no one else would dare approach me for the rest of the day. And that was the day, my love, when I took my raincoat to the cleaners.

*A blood test result with four plusses (++++) indicates syphilis

Carnations and Tomato Juice

. . .

It's early in the morning, in a little copse of pines. The bees are humming, the mosquitoes buzzing, the birds trilling. It's dark in here, dark as sunglasses, except for the dappled sunlight filtering down through the trees. And just over there, lapping up against the shore, a little patch of sea. It's just a shade darker than the sky . . . And now I am thinking of the villagers who live there. Once upon a time I discovered from books that if I learned to love people, and to delight in nature and in the world by traveling this long road, I would, the books said, learn to love life itself. But I no longer love people by the book. And neither do I have time for the four holy texts or the great tomes of science. It's fables I learn from, and stories. Poetry and fiction – those are my sciences. But if you wanted to know how I learned to loathe the servant who leaps upon his master to whisk away his luggage the moment he steps off the boat, or how I came to understand that the man who springs out of bed at six-thirty every morning to battle the elements isn't actually working – well, these were things I taught myself. But should that man choose to linger in bed one morning – well, he can spend the rest of the day trying to fool people for all I care. What difference does it make? His thick wad of banknotes don't add up to a single coin in my eyes, not a single coin.

I know which people to respect these days. I know which ones to love. Then there are those who've been on my mind for days now (but let's not say that he "occupied" my thoughts).

In the village they call him Mustafa the Blind. One of his eyes is skewed to the left. On the right side of this eye there's a dark red lump of flesh where the white of his eye meets the lid. Was he born like that? Did something get caught in his eye when he was a child? This weak eye is shinier than the other, and darker, too. There's more life in it. More wit. It makes me think of a hunchback. How strange. People dismiss hunchbacks as ugly, when in fact they're charming and warm-hearted, every last one of them. They make the dearest friends. Oh, how much I adore them!

So there you have it. Mustafa the Blind. On one side of his face, an eye with the soul of a hunchback, beckoning and rejoicing, while the eye on the other side of his face is plain and old. It puts on airs. It cowers with shame. But there is never any light in it.

Mustafa the Blind tends gardens. He takes daily jobs: he plasters cisterns, fixes roofs, digs wells, that kind of work.

Few people live on the southern side of our village. It's really no more than a great tangle of briar, wild oak, arbutus, and shrubs that think they're trees. The unruly patch belongs to the Fino Church. A wild-eyed and unshaven giant of a priest makes a great show of claiming the land as his. He could, I imagine, have rented it out for some pittance, but he never got around to it. In the meantime a forestry administrator has registered the land as a protected site. So there it sits inside that copse of pines, a tangle of weeds, shrubs, and branches too wiry to burn. Saved by the Forest Code.

And Mustafa the Blind. I don't know how he did it. But somehow he managed to tame a part of it – the part that went down to the sea. He paid a price, of course. Do you know how he paid? With the nails on his fingers. That's how. Dig under that tangle of briars and all you'll find is stone . . . Nothing but stone. All the way down to the sea. And meanwhile, there was Mustafa, who had no choice but to spend his days working elsewhere.

But in the evenings he would retrieve his shovel from the brambles and dig and hack and weed until the sun came up the next day. He dug out one stone after another. For one winter and one summer he battled the arbutus, laurel, wild oak, and brambles, the roots and thorns and weeds, and the meddling forestry administrator. I don't think there's any other man in the village who would engage in such a savage struggle for just three furrows of land.

Cracking through a stone, he would pull out a handful of dark pink heather humus to uncover the root of a wild oak that looked like a terrifying snake. He would yank it out to find the forestry administrator standing over him. After seeing him off, he would notice that his index finger was swollen, pricked by a venomous thorn. His pickaxe would go blunt. His shovel would crack. But on he went, piling up the stones. On the soft earth next to him was a massive stone the size of a man. A mossy-faced man . . . But Mustafa gave it everything he had. His shoulders, his chest, his back, his feet, his fingernails. Mustering all his power, he vanquished the stone, smashing it to pieces. When his shovel failed, he used his hands, his fingers and his nails, scratching at the earth . . .

And then, one autumn day, we looked, and the tangle of briars was gone. The pine tree saplings were the only survivors, along with three or four arbutus bushes. Sunlight filtered through the berries and the pine needles, casting shadows over the naked earth. Some of it was olive-brown. But here and there were patches of pink and grey. Those who saw it, said:

"Tend an orchard, or accept a savage vine."

And that is how we learned that to triumph over nature, you had to fight tooth and nail, and with your blood and guts. With my own eyes I witnessed the battle unfold. I remember days when his blind eye was red with rage. I would sit myself under a pine tree at some distance and watch the cruel battle. And under my breath I'd cheer him on. Mustafa the Lion. That's what I called him. It was like watching a Roman slave pit himself against a lion, except for this: a slave could slay a lion in the quarter of an hour, but Mustafa took an entire year to conquer this beast, fueled by hope and despair.

One morning I had just settled into my usual place under the pine tree when I saw a village woman and three half-dressed children building something with a strange collection of boards, rocks, and sheet metal. It was a house. A house exposed to all the winds! The *poyraz*, and the *lodos*, and the *gündoğusu*, the *keşişleme*, the *yıldız*, and the *karayel*. Standing behind Mustafa as he divided up the three parcels of land into gardens and seedbeds was that sturdy woman, dressed in green.

"Mustafa the Lion," I said. "Did you find water?"

"There's a well down by the shore. It's salty, but it'll do. If only I could dig out a cistern here . . ."

He paused to catch his breath. I paused, in love and admiration and respect. I thought about all the millions of others like him, tilling our fields. Tilling fields the world over. Fighting the dragon with their calluses and their nails, rough-faced, one-eyed, one-armed . . .

Young ladies, one day, your future husband will send you a dark red carnation. Look at it closely, because it might be one of Mustafa's. Young men, you know those sweet and sugary tomatoes at the village market, the ones that smell like pullet apples. Slice them open and their seeds will shine like gold. Drink the bottled tomato juice at the local restaurant one day. If you find the taste divine, like the nectar that gives Greek gods eternal life, know that one of Mustafa's tomatoes was thrown into the mix.

By the Beyazıt Fountain

. . .

I'm waiting for you on one of the benches by the Beyazıt Fountain. I'm thinking what it means when someone my age feels the joyful anguish of a twenty-year-old man. It might just be that I came so late to these things. Then again, it could all be in my imagination: a heartache has its own delights, it can make a man feel young again. But that is not to say that a long summer can banish winter forever. Winter will be spectacular, burying the roads in snow. Burying the world itself under pure white meadows of death.

I'm waiting for you to come to me. When I see you at last, I will feel my heart flutter. But you will pass by without even seeing me, and I will sink back into myself, despairing, but at the same time, oddly hopeful. And there I shall stay, shut up inside myself, until all I can see is a world drenched in misery. And then I shall leave this place, to seek solace in the voices of others. I shall wander from one street market to the next, through a city you and I have made together.

Everyone in the world has passed by this fountain by now, everyone except for you. Your face was the only one I didn't see. Tears filled my eyes.

You might have thought I was a child, crying because it was a holiday, and he wanted to go on a swing.

Was it the cold that was making me shiver? Was it my nerves or was it grief? I couldn't tell. The water in the fountain was murky. The clock on the gate told me it was a few minutes past noon. The benches by the fountain were empty. What a terrible screech from the tram! I thought I recognized someone on the tram. Why did he turn around and look at me like that? Or is it just that at this hour no one ever really sits on these benches except those who have nowhere else to go. Isn't anyone in this city in love? Am I the only man in the city who is sitting on a park bench, waiting, waiting, just to catch a glimpse of his beloved?

They sat down on the bench next to mine. A woman and a man. The man turned to smile at me. I didn't feel like smiling, but a smile this warm deserved a response; he was that kind of man. So why had I refused to smile at anyone else that morning? I was waiting for you. I was still waiting for you. I was wondering why you weren't passing this way, today, at this hour . . . I was wondering, even, if you might be unwell . . .

Then I saw someone with hair like yours, and the same way of walking; and when I saw it wasn't really you, I began to worry about the real you; I began to fear the worst. Then I fell to thinking that you knew full well that I was sitting here waiting for you, and so had chosen to go out through the other gate. But I quickly dispelled the paranoia. How important could I be?

But what if you were ill?

That really happened once. As soon as I heard, I raced to your bedside. You opened your eyes. There was sweat on your brow. Two strands of light blonde hair stuck to your forehead. You said, "The fever's not dropping." I raced back into the city. I came back with medicine from the black market. You got better. We walked the length of the pier together. You were fresh-faced, flushed. You were smiling. You teased me. You ran away from me and I couldn't catch you. God forbid. Keep fevers at bay!

These were the thoughts that raced through my mind after the man on the next bench smiled at me. So it took me a few seconds to respond. But I must have made up for lost time. Because now the man stood up and came over.

"What's the name of that mosque?"

Would you believe it if I said I couldn't remember the name? My mind was still with you. No, you hadn't come down with another fever, thank God – nothing as dire as that! I could almost see you moving through the back streets to avoid me. A wave of despair crashed over me. But I can never stay angry at you . . . No, I'm angry at the world. I'm angry at my best friend . . . I'm angry at this cold spring of 1946, this month of May that feels nothing like May. I'm angry at those girls over there, and their senseless laughter. I can't stay angry at you. But if you did go off through the back streets so as not to see me, then at least you were thinking of me.

The name came back to me:

"It's Beyazıt Mosque, my friend!"

The woman stood up and came over to join us. An intense curiosity played on her face. Clearly the man had asked me an important question. And I had helped them unravel a perplexing mystery. She sat down beside us. Now it was her turn:

"So which one's Ali Sofya?"

"It's over that hill there."

I pointed to the left. But they still couldn't tell where Ali Sofya was. They just couldn't see it, exactly in the direction I was pointing. I pointed out over a maze of crossing roads, looming buildings, and shops. How would they ever find the Hagia Sophia through all of that? But there was no helping these two: it was hopeless. I could see them trying – thinking, yes, it must be over there. Finally the man said:

"It must be a long way away."

"No, it's not that far," I said.

I put the man at over fifty. His face was deeply wrinkled and the color of earth.

"I brought this one back from the village with me," he now said.

He pointed to the woman beside him. Her head was covered in a modest headscarf, and her face was as crinkly as a caramel-covered rice pudding, which here and there caught the shimmering light. She had little eyes, sparkling white teeth and high cheekbones, and I thought I caught the scent of milk. What a lively, rosy face she had; what wonderful blood she must have, running through those veins . . .

"This one here's never been to Istanbul before. She's having a good look around, really enjoying herself, she can't stop smiling. She's having a fine time, if I say so myself. We're from Lüleburgaz. I've been to Istanbul a few times, but this one's never been before. I'm taking her around to all the mosques."

"You should see Taksim, too."

"Oh, yes. We'll see Beyoğlu too, right? That's before you get to Taksim, right?"

"That's right."

"Should we take the tram?"

"Why not!"

"But we also want to take the Tünel."

"It's closed, it's out of service."

"No . . . so the Tünel's closed, eh? That's a shame – for me as well as her."

The woman held out something wrapped in newspaper:

"Copper's much cheaper these days. We got this for a good price."

"How much did you pay?"

"What did we pay again? Per kilo it was . . . We got this for four hundred fifty *kuruş*. But no, wait a minute, we paid three fifty in the end. That's not much, is it?"

"We paid three hundred and twenty. It was seven hundred grams."

"You gave them five lira. What did the coppersmith give you back?"

They did the math. First they couldn't agree. Then they did. They'd bought the dish for three hundred and ten *kuruş*.

My eyes were still fixed on the road you usually walked along. Now that their math lesson was over, the couple next to me had turned to look at the fountain. By now I'd lost all hope of seeing you. So I was thinking of going after you. Finding you and saying: "Now look, listen to me please? For once just let me be honest with you. You don't ever let me speak my mind. You don't ever tell me what I need to hear. So if you could just stay calm for a moment and let me explain . . ."

"Does the water come bubbling up from the earth?"

"Oh, come now. This isn't a natural spring, my dear fellow. They pump in city water, through a pipe."

The man turned to the woman:

"They use pipes to fill it up. They lay down pipes along the bottom. You see?"

Then to me:

"But then . . . well . . . the water bubbles up?"

"On holidays or when the weather's warm . . . But it's cold now so it's not running."

To the woman:

"It's not bubbling because it's cold. You see? They bubble it up in the hot weather to cool people off . . ."

He turned to me:

"OK but . . . then they throw plastic balls on top and the water keeps the balls up in the air, keeps tossing them up in the air. That's what they do, right?"

He must be in his fifties, she's not much younger . . . And here they are, prattling about fountains and balls . . . They have more of the child in them than I do. I'm happy to be free of the pain of not seeing you; I feel fine now, absolutely fine. The woman leans over, listening. We talk about Taksim, other mosques, the city squares, the Bosphorus, the Maiden's Tower. Then the conversation dries up. We are silent for a while. I begin to search for a line of poetry to recite to you. A line about rainy weather, mountain roads, mules, bells . . . it must be out there, somewhere – don't such things exist?

Now the man is telling the woman about the Maiden's Tower, the Haydarpaşa Train Station, the Selimiye Barracks . . .

Then the three of us fall silent again, as if to mull over the important things we've just discussed. Except, for me, there's no doubt about it. There cannot be a thought I'm not ready to entertain. I can see you coming through the gate. Running over to me. I can see us arm in arm.

Just then the man says:

"Does the water freeze in winter?"

What can I say to that? I feel my sadness leave me again:

"It freezes," I say. "It freezes and the children skate on it."

He turns to the woman:

"He says it freezes in the winter, children skate on it."

What do you think, my love? Does the Beyazıt Fountain freeze over in the winter? Anyway, that's what I told Sergeant Murtaza and his wife Hacer Ana. Yes, I said, it freezes over.

Rage: A Human Habit

. . .

I tied him up tight, hand and foot. I sat him down in the corner. His eyes were flashing. He was shaking, rocking with rage. His face was yellow. But I was certain it wasn't fear that did that. It was fury, pure fury. There was no point, though, in making him angry. But that wasn't because I feared he might do something. Or pounce on me, if I untied him. That rage would dissolve the moment I set him free. What about me, though? I wasn't about to give up on him. I liked seeing him cornered, with nowhere to go.

"What's it to you, anyway? What's it to you?" He was screaming.

"What's it to *me*?" I raged. "You're asking what this means to *me*? Look around you. Every house and garden in this city is in danger. No one can sleep easy . . ."

I knew I was exaggerating, but I kept going.

"Come on now, it's not as bad as all that," he managed to say.

I hit right back at him.

"You say it's not so bad, but just by saying that, you're admitting how bad you really are," I said. Of course, it doesn't look so bad to you. Just think of the other side of the coin for a minute: a coal man's summer, an iceman's winter. Skiing down a summer slope, swimming in a winter sea. . . ." My imagination ran out.

"So look," I said instead. "You have no right. That's why tying you up is – "

"Set me free!" he screamed. "Set me free!"

"Do you repent?" I asked.

I knew he couldn't. He didn't have it in him to pretend. He calmed down:

"You're exaggerating, sir," he said.

For a while neither of us spoke. He saw now that I was not going to waver. He began to plead with me. He was sorry. May God make me an Arab if I ever do this again!

I pretended to think it over. Then I gave him my most poisonous smile:

"You think I'm going to fall for that?" I said. "You don't mean a word you say. You're a liar. A chicken ass! Don't think you can hide from me! You don't feel any remorse – you can't."

I stopped. I glared down at him.

"Don't you know lying is wrong?" I said.

"Yes, you're right. It's wrong," he said. "But you're being too hard on me. You know as well as I do this is something you can't promise not to do again."

"A sinner repents," I said.

"What do I know about sin?" he replied.

"You're evil," I said. "Pure evil."

"Huh! Now you're talking. Tell me what makes this evil."

I gave a few examples. He wasn't convinced. He was determined to prove to me there was nothing evil in this.

"Evil," he said. "You keep calling it evil. But when will you understand that you're just masking real evil, and with all these excuses you're only setting it up," he said. Then he went on, "In the past I felt like you didn't know what you were doing and I knew you had a pure heart. But here's what I can see: you're masking the really big evil here, masking it with these little, innocent evils," he said, and so the preaching began.

I shut him up.

My exact words were: "Shut up, dog. Shut up and tell me exactly what you think the really big evil is."

"The really big evil is injustice."

"And we who feel wronged . . ."

"Look who's so high and mighty! But you have a soft spot for pickpockets and thieves. Even murderers are better than me in your eyes. You fear them. When they've paid their dues, when they're back on the streets and walk back into the coffeehouse, you stand up to greet them. Oh, I've seen plenty of that with my own eyes – mayors and rich men and bigwigs, standing up like that in coffeehouses, for murderers . . ."

"Stop spouting nonsense," I said. "Take a good long look at yourself instead."

"I'm not doing anyone any harm," he said. "If I knew I was doing harm . . ."

"With this sort of thing, there's no difference between knowing and not knowing," I said.

But now he was past listening:

"By inventing all these small evils, you've turned the great evil, the real powerhouse evil into *desperation*. But in my world everything is unjust, everywhere we turn, there's evil, a great powerhouse of evil. And now you're attacking my desperation, my only hope, my only source of pleasure, my only joy, my only . . ."

"Your only sin."

"Yes, my only harmless, innocent sin."

"I tied you up tight, didn't I?"

With that I untied him.

"So go," I said. "Go do what you want. May God help you!"

He was gone in a flash. He was practically flying. You'd think that Chance itself was waiting breathlessly at the door. What were the odds of his avoiding instant death? One in ten, I thought. One in ten.

To cut down those odds, I ran out the back way. I didn't go to every last place he might visit, I just went to a few. Here and there I was able to reduce his chances to one in a hundred.

"A word to the wise," I said. "I've let him loose, he's outside again, he'll be here any minute."

"If he wants to come, let him come," they said.

"What do you mean, let him come? How can you say that? After all those fine words about honor and dignity? He's a menace to society!"

"You're a real piece of work," they said.

They weren't taking me seriously, I could see that. Really, they weren't equipped to take it any other way. So I played it differently, to make it worth their while to stop him.

"Of course he can come if he wants to," I said. "The point is to torment him, keep him from taking any pleasure from it."

"He has money, so why shouldn't we take it from him?" they said.

"As if!" I said. "As if the pleasure he gets can be measured in money!"

"Pleasure?"

I was taken aback when they said that. But that's the way it is . . . He and I were the only ones who understood why the pleasure they gave him was more valuable than money. Or was I just like him, without knowing? By causing him pain, was I only torturing myself? I didn't want to think about that for too long and swatted the thought away, like a fly. Instead I thought about what a great pleasure it brought me, to do him harm.

"No," I said. "That's just how it looks to you. For me, and for him, money has no value, next to the beautiful things you'll give him."

"So what are you asking here? What do you want us to do?" they asked.

"If you listen to me," I said, "you can have your money, and still deny him his pleasure."

"How?" they asked.

"How? It's easy. He'll come in. Come over. The things he's after are innocent enough: friendship, safety, intimacy, a bit of conversation . . . And you make as if you have all that to offer. The thing he wants more than anything, though – no doubt about it – he'll save that for last. But because you already know, you can look like you might know, or might not. And he'll think he has the trump card in his hand all this time, and just when he's about to play it, he'll see that he has no trump card, that the card in his hand is blank, while you hold a double trump in your hand. But you will have made every humanly possible sacrifice. There's no harm in that."

"What's the point of all this?"

"The point of it is to get him to hate everything around him – you, himself, the world, money, the street, everything on earth – the moment he sees it, the moment he tastes it."

"And then?"

"And then it's over the rainbow . . . And then you . . ."

"All right. All right! You've said enough. We'll do what you want," they said.

He came home that evening, of his own accord. He threw himself into the same corner where I'd had him tied up earlier. He stretched out his legs, hid his head in his hands.

I caressed his graying hair, almost pulling on it.

"What went wrong? What put you into such a miserable state?"

"If only you had kept me in," he said. "If only you had kept me right here, bound hand and foot."

"What happened to you, darling? Come on now. Tell me what happened."

What didn't he tell me, the poor fool. They had taken my theoretical example literally, and put it into practice so well that even I was frightened by the pleasure I took from it.

"So what are you going to do now?" I said.

"You've got what you wanted. From here on in, there's no need to tie me up. From now on, I'm just sitting here. I'm going nowhere. No more chasing after pleasure. No more of that for me!"

"So. At last you've come to your senses. Good for you!" I said that but I knew full well that before morning, before the next false dawn broke, the city would be calling to him, the streets with its bright and flashing lights. By morning he would be long gone from that corner he'd curled up in, so wretched and so sore. He'd be back on the street.

Until the day I found him in that same corner, staring up at me, wide-eyed and dead.

from

A Cloud in the Sky

. . .

I could say that everything I know about this man I have on good authority, but please, don't take my word for it. There is, I think, no need to dwell on the rumors. Let me just confirm that he has a flat stomach and very long legs, with a head of golden hair, and shifty eyes. Let me also make it clear that I have no wish to imply that gossip is a wicked pastime, bringing us no joy. At the end of the day, it can enhance a reputation. We could, if we wished, imagine this man in an old-style photograph – a figure set against a background of shimmering fog. For we are not afraid.

So there he was, sitting on the low wall overlooking that vacant lot and the sea. And there, at his feet, was his dog, resting on its haunches, its front legs stretched out straight, still as a statue but for its cold, wet nose. . . Every now and then it looked up at its master and whimpered, as if to say, *let's go . . .*

The man lit a cigarette and said:

"Sit. Stay still!"

The dog stretched out its front legs and put its nose between them. It closed its eyes. A gentle breeze rustled through its yellow fur, and the man's wiry hair.

There was white mixed in with the gold. Beneath each line on his face were untold stories. Unrequited loves. Bitter heartaches. Lost looks. Lost books. Years wasted on drink and inner turmoil. Had I all the time in the world, there's no telling what I could have found there. And what if I said that those crow's feet around those blue eyes of his were not from laughing but from squinting at the sun? You'd just have to take my word for it! That said, I'm sure he utters those exact words whenever he happens to catch a glimpse of his reflection. I'm sure it's what he tells his dog. But if you asked me how I can dare to make such a claim, when not a single neighbor has ever heard him utter these words, I would urge you to forget about neighbors and think instead about postmen – a nosy postman who can't get this man out of his mind. And so there he is, in the middle of nowhere, passing the time of day with a man who has just offered him a cigarette, and saying:

"Aha! Oho! You mean that man who talks to his dog? Well, let me just tell you. The other day I took him a letter. The front door was ajar. I could hear all kinds of strange noises inside. Of course I pricked up my ears! I said to myself, 'Now, there's no one else inside but the man and his dog. Oh my God! What sort of dark business is this? Who could this man be talking to?' So I peer inside to take a look. And wouldn't you know it? He's in there talking with his dog. A Rumeli Turk, chattering away with his dog – in Greek . . ."

The man who has given him the cigarette says:

"Good God, what was he saying? Or don't you know Greek?"

"My good sir! How could I not? This is a Greek village. I've been the postman here for fifteen years. Of course I know Greek. Except . . . Forgive me, my good sir. But my throat's a little dry. You wouldn't mind stepping across there and fetching me a lemon soda? The good gentleman will be well aware that it's no easy business traipsing all over town. Let me confirm that officially, my good sir. There are evenings when I pull off my shoes to find my feet aren't the ones I left with in the morning. They're twice the original size . . . Twice at least! Oh dear! All the same . . . Ah, what a pig! This soda's ice cold! It's not always like that . . . So where was I? Oh, so I peered inside and listened: 'You,' he said, 'you think I'm old, don't you?' And then he says, 'No, of course you don't. I know you and you know me. So let me ask you . . . Do I ever tire of stomping over these hills and dales? You could try and tell me I'd had my fair share of laughter. You could point at all those wrinkles around my eyes . . . and around my lips . . . But you wouldn't, my fine friend. Would you? I can't say I never laughed, because I have. But I have never *truly* laughed. Not from the bottom of my heart. Whenever that urge comes to me, I recall something my mother liked to say: 'Laugh from the bottom of your heart and you shall weep as many tears.' I simply can't laugh the way I want to. You know how people smile when they meet someone they know. Well, that's the best I've ever managed, in my happiest moments. If I hold back my smiles when I greet people, it's because I'm afraid they might lead me to cry. But I'm rambling, dear friend! All I meant to say was that those crow's feet aren't from tears or laughter. They're from that sun up there . . . Up there in the sky. You know how I wander about all day under the sun. Now look closely right here. There are more wrinkles around my left eye, aren't there? That's because the squint in that eye is stronger. Because the eye itself is more sensitive to light. It's been that way since the day I was born. The other eye's fine, thank God. So I can get by. Otherwise I'd have to wear a monocle. Imagine that, my friend. A one-eyed dandy!"

Could we imagine the postman uttering the very words I have just set down on paper? I ask because he never did. But just imagine that he had. Imagine his voice, hissing like a serpent. Imagine the cold, jaundiced glint in his lying eyes. Imagine all that and you can see the listener bidding the postman goodbye, and going off to repeat the story, and not just the story, but the fidgeting. The hissing voice. The gaze. That much you would agree. So now that I am ready to write what remains of this story – beyond the episode that cost me a cigarette and a lemon soda – allow me to indulge in a modest preamble, in which I'll reveal the secrets of my trade. From now on, I shall write in such a way as to stir you to ask, "And how do you know all this?" How I know such things I decline to say. But I can't stop myself from saying this: maybe I live with this man. Though I won't say that maybe he's me. Say if I were to write, "Alone in his room, he scratched his head." You might ask me how I knew that, or if I had seen him do it. Or if I were to say, "He wakes up in the morning with a heavy heart." What a ridiculous line that would be! You might ask, "Are you this man? Stop playing games! Enough! How could you ever know how the bastard feels?" You have every right to lose patience . . . Please forgive me. I shall make the same mistake many times over in the story I am about to tell. I can no longer remember if I mentioned the remarkable affinity I feel for this man. But there is one last point I'd like to make before proceeding to the heart of the matter; though this man is a kindred spirit, I have no real connection to him. I am simply setting down what our inquisitive postman and others like him have told me. So if that much is clear . . .

Like the postman said, I don't think he's avoiding people. But surely there's a reason he spends so much time alone . . . He himself might not know the reason why. As the postman pointed out, he doesn't seem cut out for life on an island, surrounded by water on all sides. He belongs in the city, surrounded by throngs. No one here in this little place would ever talk to such a man, let alone drink rakı with him; people might befriend him early on, just to learn a bit about him, but then they would peel away, leaving him alone with his dog. No one bothers him. So let's leave behind what the postman had to say and turn to the barber:

"It's love that did this to him."

So what's this man's problem? You cannot pretend he's just like you or me. The fact of the matter is that this man talks to his dog! But then again, we hear of people speaking to walls, and their personal effects, to their dreams, beds, and mirrors. Some even talk to their neckties. Young girls speak to their hope chests. Young men speak to their own bodies as they make love. We know all this.

Then we have the poets speaking to women with no names, conversing with the stars and the winds, addressing lakes and distant lands and migrant birds and clouds drifting two thousand meters up in the sky. We have the fishermen, prattling away to their boats and rods and fish . . . but in these parts, when a man speaks with his dog, he becomes the object of ignominious gossip. Personally, I am not convinced that love made this man the way he is. For me, there's nothing unnatural about him at all! But I am alone in this, I regret to say... No doubt the man's not quite in his right mind . . . Here is my theory, for what it's worth: people don't much mind that he talks to his dog. What bothers them is his reluctance to speak to anyone else. And well, how shall I put this? These people spend their lives pouring their hearts out to each other. When anyone backs away from them, they thirst for answers . . .

Back to the rumors.

It seems that he owns two stores in the city and that he collects rent. He keeps the books for a tradesman involved in some mysterious business located who knows where. This tradesman is cut from the same cloth: he doesn't speak much, shuns society; and he's also a bachelor. They rarely say more than hello and goodbye.

Then there is this story:

They say that once upon a time there was a young woman he'd chat with on the ferry. There are even those who claim to have heard this eighteen-year-old girl speaking intimately with this man who was more than twice her age. They even heard him singing to her. Word finally reached the young girl's father: he gave her a stern warning, and there the friendship stopped. Sometimes they would both end up on the last boat back to the islands, but now the poor girl goes straight back to sit with her two friends. After wandering along the decks for a spell, he heads to the prow, there to whistle a soft folk song. Though he was known for never greeting anyone, he would always greet this girl, and – strange as it might sound – she would greet him . . .

But the fact is, they never really exchanged more than a few words: "Hello," and "How are you?" and, "I hope all is well with you."

So that's all the gossip I have on the man. That's all anyone knows. But there is one creature on this earth who could reveal to us his deepest secrets. And that, my friends, is his little dog. A bright-eyed dog with a wet nose, and a golden coat that flutters in the wind . . . Now this dog belongs to him, not me. I mention him here only to make a point. Unless the dog is a figment of my imagination, at least in part? The fact is that the poor man will never manage to make the small creature understand how he lost his illusions, and let his fears get the better of him, to be left all alone. Dogs are not, and never will be, creatures of the word. If they want to show their owners some affection, they lick their hands and dash about wagging their tails. But here's what I know from my imaginary dog:

"He got up early that morning. I heard a soft whistling, and I raced over to him . . ."

I suppose if I let the dog tell the rest of my story things would take a turn for the worse . . . The long and the short of it is that I decided one day to make friends with the man who sat on that low wall every evening, smoking his cigarettes, lost to his own thoughts. I walked over to him:

"*Beyefendi*," I said. "If you don't mind . . ."

"Oh, but of course, *efendim*, please sit down."

I lit a cigarette. I sat down beside him. As I stroked his dog, he felt the need to speak first:

"You're an animal lover?"

"*Beyefendi*, I adore them."

"Truth is I was never very fond of them. But I'm quite used to them now. This one's mother once belonged to an old lady who ran the little hotel I used to live in. Long before this one was ever born. The poor woman died. Her dog stayed with me from then on. I was very fond of that lady. Then some time passed. The dog died. It was a girl. This one here's a boy. Back then someone wanted to take him away and I was going to give him up. But I kept him as a memory of his mother . . ."

That evening we didn't share anything more interesting than this. Neither of us understood politics, nor did we have any interest in the subject. We could do little more than confirm each other's beliefs: which is, of course, to say we talked politics. When I got home that evening, I couldn't understand why the postman was so interested in this fellow. He was the most ordinary man in the world. Even the wealthy shopkeeper who lived across the road was more interesting than him. Wouldn't you agree? His thoughts are mired in olive oil, green beans, flour, and garbanzo beans; he's rolling in money, his children go to the famous schools and take dancing lessons and wear expensive clothes . . . And his daughter – she speaks such beautiful English! She graduated from a private college, no small feat! How pleased that's made her father! How proud she's made him! He's more than happy to tell you the whole story: how he came here all the way from Chios to work as an errand boy at a corner shop, how in time he took over the business, how the owner continued to stop by to see him now and then, and how one day he offered his own daughter's hand in marriage . . . His life, as he tells it, has been one long, thrilling ascent. Up and up he went, achieving one miracle after another. But how could people seeing only his tiny little shop in the fish market have any concept of the enormous storehouse just below? The Kurd at the door is impenetrable. The same could be said of the bleak iron shutters of the Byzantine warehouses beyond. Everything's there in that tangled, medieval labyrinth where the carts pile up one on top of the other and porters walk along dark, oily conveyor belts, shouting as they go. The shopkeeper is fair-skinned. But his wife is olive-skinned. So, can that blond and honey-eyed son really be hers? He has a classic Grecian nose. And broad shoulders. He reminds his father of Alexander the Great. Yani Efendi is a well-educated man. He adores his son. His daughter, too. He's so very proud of her English. But in Greece they are dying of hunger. In the coffeehouse he seems despondent. At home with his wife, he's driven to tears. Sipping his coffee, he says, "Why not buy five, ten kilos more than we need and put them to one side, my sweet Eleni. You just never know!"

But that's as far as I can take Yani Efendi's life story . . . My fault entirely! As tired as I was, I still managed to retrace his steps. I was like Balzac, plotting the life of a perfumer. But you can't really expect me to burst into the man's home and compose a great novel, rattling off details of a place I've never seen.

But never mind. What I meant to say was that Yani Efendi had me so intrigued for a time that I forgot about the other one, the man with the dog, who once upon a time had kept everyone guessing – even me. Had I cared to do so, I could have joined him any evening on that little wall and drawn him into yet another tiresome conversation, from which I might have learned all manner of things. But no, I've had my fill of oddballs. No good can come of them! I'm saving myself for the ones who rejoice in life! This man hardly *has* a life . . . He has no one but his dog. He speaks to his dog and no one else. Bearing that in mind, let's return to the postman's observations:

"My good sir, this man has never once treated another man to a coffee. But please, let's step into this gazino here and have a cup of coffee together. Oh, the things I could tell you about him . . . You could never imagine . . ."

"Some other time, some other time!"

I couldn't be less interested. It's Yani Efendi I want to know about now. I've just become friends with his son.

But five days on, he's beginning to wear on me. He does have his charms, if only he'd stop talking! Now I can talk as much as any man about films and dances and poker games and women's legs. But with this one, it's the same every night! There's no harm in it, I know. But one evening he takes it upon himself to mimic a matinee idol, a certain John Payne. Now I might enjoy speaking to the man himself, were I in America, but what business does this John Payne have, talking to me in Istanbul? That was our final conversation. These days, when we see each other, we just exchange a few laughs. In a few days, we won't even do that . . . Meanwhile I've more or less given up on the idea of writing about the life of Yani Efendi. I've gone back to the man and his dog. Good that I took a long break from him. His shyness must have got the better of him that first time. But this time he even offered me a cigarette. And then, just for my sake, he scolded his dog:

"I was really beginning to worry about you. Where have you been, my friend? You just disappeared."

"Just a little cold, but it kept me in bed for the week, *beyefendi*!"

"You're feeling better now, I hope?"

Then he told me how he once caught a cold that simply wouldn't go away. But even so, he couldn't keep himself out of the sea, and so he'd spent the entire summer sniffling. Here was this man, who'd told his own dog he never laughed. But today he couldn't stop! It seemed to me the dog was flashing him a funny look: no doubt the result of a long chat with the postman!

I suppose it's time I told you more about the postman. As I've already said, I found few failings in him, beyond his habit of ferreting out other people's secrets – tidbits about their little failings and predilections, the sorts of things that should never go beyond four walls.

Is the postman a good man or is he not? What do I care, either way?

All that matters is that I can't help liking him, even though he gets on my nerves. He has this infuriating habit of planting himself three paces behind me, and staying put. No chance of talking to anyone else after that. There is little I have to say to the world that I can't say loud and clear, but when I see this postman sitting there, drinking in my every word, I can't help myself. I fly into a rage. I forget whatever it was I wanted to say. Whatever it was, I just wanted to say it slowly. And then I remind myself: "The bastard can take two words out of a sentence and add twenty new ones, and come up with a whole story, so watch out!"

This is, in fact, what happened: We have a mutual friend named Ahmet. He rents a room for the summer season from Mademoiselle Katina. The other night he went for a swim. Two friends of his were speaking about it just a couple of feet away from the postman:

"You know Ahmet from Katina's house, well he went for a swim in the sea last night despite all that wind. He told us to come in too but . . ."

From this the postman extracted three things exactly: "Katina, Ahmet, last night . . ." And this is what he said to his barber:

"Now hello there, barber! How about helping me get rid of this rubble? But listen to what I have to tell you. You know Ahmet, who stays in one of those houses on the hill? Last night he took off in a rowboat with none other than Katinaki, the daughter of the famous chocolatier. They rowed all the way over to Heybeliada. Then they hopped into a phaeton and it was off to Çamlımanı! I watched them from that promontory. First I saw them rowing across the channel. Then, a little later, I watched them make their way along the lengthy shore road in a lit carriage. I swear I saw that phaeton with my own two eyes. The driver was waiting for them in Abbaspaşa. Oh! How sweet it must have been, Barba. You'll remember it rained yesterday. You know how sweet it smells in that pine forest after it rains! But who will ever know the scent of lavender in Katinaki's hair? Oh lord! Barba, it's enough to drive a man mad! As for this Ahmet Efendi, he's not bad looking himself, is he? What eyes he has! Thin as a whip, too! Let's hope he wasn't too hard on that delicate Katinaki!"

So that was the story that the postman spun. I can only admire his knack for making a story out of nothing because serious writers like me can only dream of it.

Let me say what I think is underneath it all:

On the surface, it might look as if he is divulging great secrets in exchange for small favors – a tea here and a soda there. A shave, a small glass of rakı, a bunch of grapes . . . But if you ask me, these trifles are not what keep him serving up secrets. I figured this out when I noticed that if he could find no one else to confide in, he would go to Zafiri, who is a quiet soul and hates gossip and cannot afford a coffee for himself, let alone anyone else, and can barely speak Turkish. Or he'll go and sit with Zeynel Efendi, the retired ticket salesman, who is as quiet as Zafiri and just as disdainful of gossip.

The postman hungers after secrets because he longs to grasp the world he can see only in his imagination.

And there are times, many times, when I think he goes too far. First he strings up the dirty laundry, and then comes the laundry that he's soiled himself. The innocent truth is never enough for him. Never – but then what are we to do? He's the one who has to pay the price. It's a risky business, building a house of lies, even if it sits on a foundation of facts . . . I'd end up forgetting what the postman's said about whom, and soon I'd even forget *what* he's said, and at that point, I'd move on. As we all do, eventually. Some days, we believe what people tell us, and the next day, we don't.

I do not hide the fact that I am a writer. It's nothing to be ashamed of! But I don't like to announce it. Now if I choose to sit and write in the corner of a gazino every morning, that is why. In the old days I would go and write under a pine tree. Now I have my own table! And they bring me a coffee. Girls stroll past. I can write whatever I wish . . .

What I am trying to say is that the postman has proved very helpful!

"He sits under the pines and writes letters. . . Who knows who he's writing to . . . or what he's saying?"

But oh, the things he has inferred from stories I have written and then torn up! It shames me just to think of them. Once I nearly got into a fight over it. They all descended on me, saying, "This brute has the gall to write about our lives! Who does the bastard think he is?"

I have gone on far too long about the postman. Let's just accept him as he is. Let's leave it to the others to decide if he is good or bad. But let's not smear him, since he has proven useful.

He caught up with me one morning, when I was going out for a swim:

"Look," he said, "the man with the dog! He is sending letters to his newspaper."

I looked and saw that it was indeed an envelope addressed to an assistant editor named X at a paper named Y.

Without looking up, I cried:

"Indeed it is!"

Then our eyes met. Something strange passed between us.

Turning my eyes back to the envelope, I said:

"Well it is indeed. Perhaps it's a complaint. Or a letter to the editor."

Again, our eyes met. There isn't a judge on this earth who could say who was the offender and who the accomplice, or who was provoking whom.

We ripped open the envelope. We didn't hurry to read it. First we went and got an envelope. We addressed it to the same editor, at the same paper. Then we went to the beach and settled ourselves beside a lone boulder.

On a sheet of paper folded in four, we found the following lines:

Esteemed Sir:

I am sending you this humble story as a contribution to your short story competition. Please feel free to publish it if you like it. With all my respect.

On another piece of paper folded in two there was this story:
(The name was lyrical, even sensual!)

Moonlight

Once upon a time I was in love. I am counting on you to understand why! How could anyone not fall in love with her! (There followed a torrid description, which we passed over quickly.) *I was living in a village on the other side of the Sea of Marmara. Every evening, we'd travel back together. I won't lie to you. My feelings for her were not entirely normal. By which I mean to say they were not as they should have been. When we fall in love, we should feel as if we've been struck by lightning. We should resolve to do whatever it takes, to win our beloved's heart. A love like this has its charms, but it's not for me. First I need a little bit of encouragement. After that, things are easier. Until I am again encouraged, and then I feel as if I've been caught in a trap, and from then on, I am trying to escape. Until there is a third bit of encouragement. Then it's all over. I'm madly in love.*

And now it had happened once again. The second time I saw her, I knew I was heading for parts unknown. Never again would I see the place of my birth or the beloved country where I had made my life. A great sadness fell over me. I almost said an "indescribable sadness," but here I am, describing it.

Everyone and everything I loved was falling away: my language, my homeland, my mother, my father, my house, my garden, and my friends. And oh, the tears I shed as they gathered round me, saying, "You're leaving us! How can you do this to us? Shame on you! Can it be true? Are you really going to abandon us, just like this? We never expected this of you . . . Are you really leaving us? Are you never coming back? Are you actually leaving us for . . . her? For this woman? Take a good look at her now. Take a good, long look. You won't regret it!"

The ferry cuts through the calm waters, the stars trail behind. The passengers become their own shadows. And on we sail. I want the journey to go on forever. I pay no heed to the warnings my loved ones keep whispering in my ears.

Who first introduced us, I cannot say. Neither can I say how this came about, or on what pretext. I've forgotten everything and everyone but her. Were there stars in the sky above her? Ships in the sea? . . . Even the sun did not exist, because it wasn't there that night. Even the moon! This pale slip of a shadow, hardly visible by day had only been with us for fifteen days – and how could we be sure that it existed at all? There were moments when I forgot even this. How beautiful the face of this earth! Such lies it conjures up! Lies can be made of all the things we know to be true – the moon, the stars, and birds, and whistles, and violins, and ships! Oh, such beauties we can find on the face of the earth! And oh, my beloved! And oh, the things I could do, if she and the world were both mine! The third time, I sought her out. She half recognized me, half didn't. I was crushed. The fourth time, I gave her a casual wave, in passing. But inside I was churning, like a river joining the sea. "Let it go," I told myself. "Just keep your distance." The fifth time our paths crossed, I didn't even say hello.

I went up to sit at the bow. The moon that night was lovely. Was it full? I'm not sure. All I can remember is that there was the moon, and my beloved. How flat those two words are. But what a history they carry. It could only have been a moonlit night when Adam first fell in love with Eve. There were many more to come in the centuries that followed! But there is no one on this earth who could have been unhappier than I was on that moonlit night. Not even the lover caught in the midday sun. Not even the man standing at his window, puffing miserably at his cigarette. The word itself does not begin to describe it. But never mind. There's no need to look for a better one. A man in the moonlight is a man walking the thin line between misery and bliss. Did you know, for instance, that love has two sides, like the moon itself? Think, perchance, of the lover who commits suicide on a moonlit night. He's a happy man! Miserable enough to find the joy in death, but happy in the knowledge of the joy that death will bring! ("This part's awful!" I said to the postman.) On the night in question, that was precisely my line of thinking. In my mind, I could feel death's cold lips pressing down on me. But here, before me, was a woman with warm lips, and a body smooth as marble. "Hello," she said. She sat down beside me. "How are you doing?"

"Terrible," I said.

"What's wrong?"

"Nothing. Honestly, nothing at all. Oh, who knows. Who can say?"

We fell silent.

When she finally spoke, she seemed to have come closer.

"What's there, on the surface of the moon?" she asked.

"On the moon?" I said.

I gave it some thought. Then I told her whatever I could remember from school.

"There's nothing on the moon . . . It's empty, meaningless, dead . . . There is no atmosphere, nothing that can support life. Even the light we see up there is false. It doesn't radiate its own light . . . What you see is a reflection of the sun's light . . . No, there's nothing there . . . Nothing . . . It's cold, or maybe it's not even that . . . Where there is no atmosphere, can there even be such a thing as heat, or cold?"

"So there's no life on the moon?"

"There's no air, as I just said!"

"Fine. But how about if you took your own oxygen?"

"Look, that part I don't know. Maybe you could last for a few hours, or a few days . . . It might be possible to stay there long enough to see a bit of the place, and satisfy your curiosity . . ."

She looked up at the moon. It felt as if she were resting her head on my shoulder. Or maybe it was the moonlight that made me believe this was so.

I succumbed to the light:

"My lovely," I said. "Have you taken leave of your senses? How could there be

anyone up there living on the moon? The only ones who can live there are lovers.
They meet for an evening, and two become one. And then they fly up to the moon
together. And most of them get there. If I were to take hold of you, if you and I were
to fall to the bottom of the sea, never to return, a host of other creatures would come
to our rescue and fly us straight up."

What a lovely laugh she had. I had taken everything I'd learned in geography
class and turned it on its head. And that was how I came to find the courage to
hold my beloved's hand.

I managed not to laugh. The postman laughed a great deal. But something
in his face had changed. He was no longer curious. He no longer wished
to know what secrets lurked in people's hearts. He put it like this:

"They're all alike. But I used to think that the man with the dog was different. There were things about him that seemed unique. Oh, the tragedies
I dreamed up for him! He certainly kept me guessing. When all it was was
love. But I just couldn't see it – how a man who kept his own company and
talked only to his dog could be like you or me. Now I can read the letters
I carry without even opening them. I already know them all by heart."

And off he went up the hill.

The Last Birds

. . .

Winter came with the winds – the *poyraz* and the *yıldız poyraz*, the *maestro*, and the *dramaduna*, the *gündoğusu*, the *karayel*, and the *batı karayel*. It took up residence on one side of the island while summer lingered on the other, a wistful nomad who had yet to gather up her things. I have no wish to sing my own praises, but I do believe I am the only man on the island who fully appreciates this fresh-faced beauty as she wavers (passport in one hand, a pouch of gold pieces in the other) between staying and going.

All around me, they were making their preparations for six or seven months of cold. But I, in my idleness, was playing hide and seek with my nomad. Whenever I caught up with her, I held her in my arms. Sometimes she hid in the shade of a pine. Sometimes I would find her in the grass, next to a bush – as radiant as if she had never left.

On this side of the island, where summer is so slow to close her tattered bundles, the only structure standing is a little coffeehouse.

It is no larger than a small balcony, just five or ten meters above a quiet bay. Ants still wander over its wooden tables. Flies perch on the edges of coffee cups. There isn't a sound. Then from somewhere in the sky comes the humming of a plane. I only imagine the passengers as I write these lines now. There were other planes, earlier on. But this is the first time I've stopped to think about the passengers who are soon to disembark at Yeşilköy, who may already have done so by the time I finish these two lines.

The proprietor is a surly man, more like a cantankerous civil servant than the proprietor of a coffeehouse. It's the last job in the world he would have chosen, but he was in poor health and his doctors told him to take it easy. I have very different reasons: I stayed away from the job because I couldn't find the right coffeehouse. What I had in mind was a coffeehouse in the country, or a village. With only three or four regulars ... I can't think of a more beautiful life. What could be more beautiful than a life spanning fifty or sixty years, if it began and ended in such a place?

The underwear strung up between two trees will never dry in this warm weather. It's overcast and still. A cat is up on the tabletop. Will it keep grumbling at my dog? Those holey socks draped over the chairs are as dark as cherry stones ... The vine leaves are greener than ever. The ones in our garden are already dry.

The sea is racing off to the Bozburun Peninsula. What part of Istanbul is that, hovering in the distance? Why is there no sound?

Another plane flies overhead. Our island must be underneath a flight path – they are always going right over us, or just to the left. The cat's stopped grumbling. My dog's eyes are closed. Now I can hear the crows. Time was when birds would flock to the island at this time of year. They'd fill the air with their chirping. They'd swarm in flocks from tree to tree.

For two years now, we haven't seen them.

Or have they come and gone without my knowing?

Toward autumn I'd see families – all sorts – heading toward the highest hill on the island with cages in their hands. I'd shudder at the sight.

The older ones carried strange, shit-colored clubs.

When they reached the edge of a green meadow, they'd set down their cage. Inside was a decoy bird. Placing the cage beneath a little tree, they'd smear birdlime all over its branches. The wild birds would hear the decoy's lonely cry – for friendship, for company – and swoop down to help, while that bunch of bruisers kept watch from the shade of a neighboring tree. Then slowly they'd come back out into the open to walk toward the cage, the decoy, and the swarms of wild birds. Four or five would manage to break free of the birdlime and while they were flying off to be caught on yet another patch of lime, these men would gather up their quarry. Each bird a miracle of nature. Each yielding no more than a drop of flesh. Then and there, they'd break their necks with their teeth. And then pluck them alive.

There was one in particular, I'll always remember him. This one brought boys with him to do the job. He'd prepare the birdlime on Saturday night . . . The bastard's name was Konstantin. He had an office in Galata. A grain store. He was a broad-chested man, with thick, hairy wrists; his smile was oily and unctuous; his nose was covered with moles and his nostrils flared. A shock of unruly hair, and mincing footsteps.

If only you could see him, wrapping his fingers around those golden brown feathers, and sinking his glittering chrome teeth into the bird's neck. Already tasting the pilaf he would sprinkle with its drop of flesh.

He was a calm and humble man. He didn't flaunt his wealth. His neighbors liked him and all that. He never meddled in their affairs. Never gossiped. If you saw him pitter-pattering off to work of a morning, or stepping off the ferryboat of an evening, swinging his heavy string bag, you'd find nothing amiss in his massive frame, his casual air, his Karaman accent. His simple, if calculated, way of thinking. The simple, if endearing, jokes he told after throwing back a few glasses. In his natural state he could be any one of a thousand other people, measuring their lives on their way to work.

But in the fall he became a monster. In the space of an instant, a monster. Seated on a bench on the back deck of the 5:35 ferryboat, he would let his contented eyes travel over the surface of the sea. He would lift them to the wondrous late September sky. Then suddenly his eyes would light up. His entire face.

A swarm of dark brown specks would appear, in the sky and on the green-blue sea. They would dance to the right and left, these dark brown specks, before setting course to vanish as fast as they had come.

Konstantin Efendi would squint as he gazed in their wake. He would see where the brown specks were heading. Yes. It was the island. Looking around him, he would seek out someone he knew. Then he'd wink and point up to the sky and say:

"Our pilaf has arrived!"

If the birds passed close enough, he'd whistle through his teeth. With his thick lips, he would imitate their song. Once I saw a whole flock of them deceived. They circled around the boat before they left, detained by what they thought had been a friendly cry.

Then the weather changed. The *lodos* and the *poyraz* went to war over us, but on one warm, sweet hyacinth day in late autumn, when the wind had died down, when strips of cloud still hovered in the sky, he managed to locate an excellent decoy for his cage. He called in all the neighborhood boys. One by one they plucked the finches from the sky, and the titmice, the floryas and the odd sparrow. A thousand birds, yielding no more than 250 grams of flesh.

The birds haven't come for years now. Or maybe I just don't see them. Once I glimpsed one of those beautiful autumn days through my window. I set out wondering just where along the hillside I might find Konstantin Efendi. My blood froze when I heard the chirping of a bird. My heart stopped. But how could that be? Flying amidst the arbutus berries, the white and olive-colored clouds, the soft sunlight, and this peaceful wash of blue, a bird call can only conjure up a world of peace and poetry. Literature, art, music. Happy, understanding souls that never heed the call of greed. However far afield we travel, wherever we are in the world, a calling bird speaks one language. Konstantin Efendi is a mere hindrance. But what are we to do? The birds no longer come here. Maybe in a few years they'll be gone forever. Who knows how many Konstantin Efendis there are in the world? First it was the birds. Now it's our green spaces. The other day I stepped out onto the road as I couldn't bear to crush the grass along the sidewalk. It was one of those Konstantin Efendi days. There wasn't a bird in the sky. Before leaving home, I'd pressed a fig up against my titmouse's cage. Cracking a fig seed, he looked up at me fondly through one eye.

I'd hung the cage on a nail I'd hammered into the wall and set off. There were no birds in the sky, but there was green grass along the side of the road . . . I looked down: chunks of the grass had been torn away. A little further on I noticed four boys walking ahead. Stopping at one of the love-liest patches of green, they shoveled out a clump the size of a paving stone and tossed it into a sack.

"What are you boys doing?" I asked.

"What's it to you?" they replied.

They were just poor children, dressed in tattered clothes.

"But friends, why are you pulling up the grass?"

"Ahmet, the engineer. We're working for him."

"What are they going to do with these?"

"You know the Dutch leather merchant up there? They're landscaping his garden . . ."

"He should buy English grass and plant it, that guy's a rich bastard . . ."

"Isn't this the same as English grass?"

"Is it any better?"

"Of course, can you really find grass better than this? That's what the Dutchman says."

I ran to the police station and informed them. They supposedly took action. But the boys continued to pull up the grass here and there on the sly, and the police never did a thing about Ahmet the engineer. Even though the city council has penalties for people who pull grass out from the roadside.

They strangled the birds. They ripped up the grass. They left the roads filled with mud.

The world is changing, my friends. One day soon, there won't be a single dark-brown fleck left in the autumn sky. One day soon, there won't be a blade of mother earth's green hair left on the roadside. And children, this bodes ill for you. We older ones won't suffer. We've already known the pleasure of birds and green spaces. You're the ones who will suffer. But this story is on me.

Barba Antimos

. . .

On the wall is a picture of an English aristocrat at the Imperial Court, asking for the Queen's forgiveness. But more remarkable than that is the advertisement for "The Optimus," a modern oil lamp.

The lamp hangs from a rope on the deck of a motorboat. It sways in the wind, while fishermen underneath it heave in a net full of fish.

The canary chirps inside its cage. Restless titmice hop from one perch down to the next. The air above the stove is shimmering. Fisherman Kanari steps inside with snow on his graying blond moustache. The canary chirps again.

"Do you know Barba Antimos?"

He is a stonemason who at the age of eighty finds himself all alone on an island, far from his wife and children, as old as the pictures on the walls, and just as alive. He no longer has a boat or a fishing net, and his heart harbors no desires. His only belongings are the Priyol watch in his pocket, the red scarf around his neck, the woolen socks on his feet, and the smoke rising from his thick Maxim Gorki moustache. As for his memories – choose any year, and he'll have little to tell you. He might tell you about a wall he mended, and that would be it. It's not that he's reticent. It's just that he prefers peace and quiet. He would, I'm sure, love to spend another eighty years on this earth, building and mending and plastering walls. And dozing by the stove in the Kornil coffeehouse, while in his dreams he was already escaping through the heather to his one-room house with a loaf of bread under his arm and fresh tobacco in his case. But time is as fickle as the wind: the *lodos* gives way to the *poyraz* and then it is the turn of the *karayel*. As we drag ourselves through life, it's the rhythm of our days that seem to offer constancy. But this, too, will change. One day Barba Antimos will die.

"Barba Antimos built that wall over there," we'll say. "He used to sit there by that stove in the Kornil coffeehouse. At eighty, his eyes were still sharp and his hands still nimble enough to tuck a cigarette inside that moustache. And when he blew out the smoke, he'd puff out his cheeks." That's how we shall remember him, unless we descend into oblivion first.

Today the canary is singing, while our feet turn to ice, but one day the canary will stop singing. Apostol the Greengrocer will stop feeding rakı to Marco the Donkey. Pandeli Efendi the Milkman will no longer sit beneath that magnificent image of the British Queen with Puços, the Kornil's resident cat, in his lap. And never again will he tell us how he was sentenced to the tombs when he'd already paid his taxes or how much effort it took to change the court's decision. Knowing all this, I leave the coffeehouse. I leave behind the fragrant stink of rubber, fish, tobacco, and ink. I wend my way home. The moment I'm there, I'll get started. I shall put down on paper every year of Barba Antimos's on this earth.

The folk remedies they'd suggested for his ulcer didn't always work. There were times when he would almost complain. The lines on his face would deepen, as if to bemoan his eighty years of stoic, noble sacrifice. Blurred by sadness, his blue eyes would seem to question human company and the rule it enforced. And perhaps these were the times when the ulcer was giving him the most pain. When he spoke directly about the ulcer, the pain was probably less severe. He had been at home for days, alone with his pain. And maybe that was why he'd come out – so that he could grumble about the pain on his way down the hill, or even before he started.

"How goes it, Barba Antimos?"

"Not so good. It's quite troubling, sir. I can't sleep, can't eat. I had a little soup yesterday. But that made me . . ."

"It'll pass, Barba Antimos."

He pursed his lips. He had beautiful lips. The lips of a five-year-old child.

"The doctor at the Bulgarian hospital gave me some medicine, but it doesn't always work. You just never know."

Lean on any wall on this island. Sit on it. Climb over it or pelt it with stones. Whatever you do, you will find in it his mortar, sweat, and toil. You will find no mosaics in them, no ersatz wood or stone. He makes his walls the same way they made them two thousand years ago, and they hide secrets just as old. Greek gods, epic lovers, heroes railing against injustice. Touch a wall that Barba Antimos has made, and you touch antiquity. Pull a bag of Byzantine gold out of one of his cisterns – just three years old – and you'd be hard pressed to find an archaeologist to challenge its authenticity. Grow a boxwood vine over an arbor outside one of his cottages and it won't be long before you're expecting Socrates himself to greet you the moment you step inside. And then, one summer night, when you're sitting at your table drinking wine, you'll see Alcibiades draw his blade on Socrates and say: "Fine then, have it your way. But tell me this. How can a man live as long as you have without becoming an immortal? Why, after eighty years of gathering wisdom and unearthing secrets, and finally discovering true happiness, must he leave this world behind?"

Should you lack the confidence to guess how Socrates might have answered such a question, you hold your tongue. Instead you gaze up at the stars through the dangling grapes and then down at your glass of wine.

Then, with Homer at your side, you follow a path that winds among the walls and houses and hollowed cisterns that grace the island with nothing but good taste; you find the true path that runs from Byzantium to the simplicity and poetry of the ancient Greek world, and away from the monstrous villas of the modern age.

Barba Antimos never falters in the face of adversity. He makes just enough to get by. As long as his arms are strong, he brings beauty to everything he touches. But when his ulcer flares up, not even 250 grams of Halvah wedged in bread can bring him comfort. His gnarled and knotted muscles go limp. And all that's left of him is the light in his clear blue eyes and the smoke in his blond, Maxim Gorki moustache and his long, mortar-white hair. No one remembers what he did anymore – the houses he embellished, the walls he strengthened, the lime he covered with mortar and made beautiful with his hands.

Did he know how beautiful he made everything he touched? Would he be so humble if he did? If it had been his apprentice Hristo, we would never have heard the end of it. "Now that's one of *my* walls," he would have said. "Rip out a few stones and it'll still be standing." But Barba Antimos – he never said a thing.

Now he lives with Diyojen in one of his own houses, but every couple of days he comes down to drink milk with his old friend and compatriot, Pandeli Usta. Some mornings I see him drinking milk in Pandeli's dairy shop. Draining his glass, he smiles as if his face has been caressed by a mountain breeze. And his eyes look pure enough to drink; they look like milk. Barba Antimos never breathes a word of his sorrow. But I'll tell you.

For forty years now he has carried a secret, a bitter and unspeakable secret. For forty years now, he has been pouring his grief into his walls. And some evenings, when I lean against them, I can feel them shuddering, shaking, trembling.

The Serpent in Alemdağ

. . .

The snow had already begun to fall when we walked into the theater. When we came out the square was covered in snow. A drop fell down my neck into my shirt. I shivered.

"Get your hand out of your mouth. Don't bite your nails," I yelled, and a couple walking ahead of us turned around.

They slowed down to get a better look at my face. I felt as lonely as I always did when he was with me. He'd come on Fridays. And the pipe-smoking plaster-cast sailor would be there, waiting to greet him.

The sun on the oilskin curtain made it exactly three. When I was absolutely sure he was coming, I'd let myself doze off. When he pounded on the door like he was scrambling up it, I'd hear it in my dream. I'd jump out of bed. I'd open the door. And there he'd be, ashen-faced, and breathing through the mouth. He'd pull a cigarette off the table and light up.

The world was far away. Here there was a cabinet, a mirror, a sailor cast in plaster, a bed, another mirror, a telephone, an armchair, books, news-papers, matchsticks, cigarette butts, a stove, and a blanket. The world was far away. There were planes in the sky.

Inside were passengers. The trains were running, too. Some brute signs a piece of paper and another gives him money. An evening coolness had emerged. And now the evening *simits* had come out into the world . . .

A *simit* vendor's call floated through the room. The world was far away.

A ticket collector is stapling tickets; a man and a boy are poring over a newspaper. A strong young man is stretched out on the bench. A good-looking, powerful young man with dark eyebrows. To my right lies an emaciated creature with his hands stuffed in his pockets. The boy has stopped reading. His overcoat is rolled up under his head. He's stretched out, too. I'm in the lower cabin of a ferryboat.

It's Friday. School's out. We live on Kirazlı Mescit Street in Süleymaniye. I'm around seventeen. I can remember the pine tree at the Münir Pasha Konak. That enormous pine in the high school garden that probably burned in the fire. The frescos in oil paint on the ceilings of the Münir Pasha Konak have long since turned to smoke and ash. The bedbugs burned, too. My bed and my blanket and my tears, all burned: the pools burned; the evergreens burned; memories, those memories burned; that sunburnt boy burned; the books that brought me here, all burned.

I have to find some imitation sheepskin to sew into my overcoat.

It's Monday. I'm in the ferryboat's lower cabin again, and again it's snowing. Again Istanbul is ugly. Istanbul? Istanbul's an ugly city, a dirty city, on rainy days especially. Are other days any better? No. They're not. On other days the bridge is covered in bile. The back streets are covered in rubble and mud. The nights are like vomit. The houses turn their backs to the sun. The streets are narrow, the merchants cruel, and the rich indifferent. People are the same everywhere. Even those two asleep on the bed with the gilded frame – they're not together. They're alone.

The world is filled with loneliness. It all begins with loving another human being, and in this world, it ends the same way.

It's so beautiful, Alemdağ. So very beautiful. And at this time of day, with those trees – they're more than fifteen meters high . . . And with the waters of Taşdelen and the serpent . . . But on winter days the serpent's in its cave. Let it be. The weather's mild in Alemdağ. The sun rises through the trees' scarlet leaves. Warmth descends from the sky in bits and pieces, piling up on the rotten leaves. The Taşdelen is a thin little stream. We refresh ourselves with a jug of its water and listen to it burbling through us as we undress and wash ourselves. We frolic in the water with all the other creatures who have come to drink here: a rabbit, a serpent, a blackbird, a partridge, and a goat that has escaped from Polonezköy to toast to our health.

And when the serpent cries "Panco, Panco," the goat, the partridge, and the rabbit freeze as if they're cast in plaster. And they're white as plaster. I pull a sharp knife from my pocket and cut off a few noses; the others I slash just below the wing. Once the blood is flowing, they come to life again. They leave me and run off to Panco.

I can see Panco's smile sliding toward the scar on his angry, bloodless face. He kisses the partridge on its beak and tugs the rabbit's whiskers. A serpent coils around his wrist. He's brought a ball, a football. I'm the goalkeeper. The other goalkeeper is the serpent. The rest are stretched out over the leaves, playing in the sun. For hours they frolic. When the ball flies into our goal, the serpent and I stand to the side and watch: We're spoiling the game.

It's so beautiful, Alemdağ. So very beautiful. Istanbul is covered in mud. Its taxi drivers keep driving through puddles, heedlessly splashing water over pedestrians. And heedlessly, the snow keeps seeping inside us.

A woman hurls a cat from the fifth floor. A woman and a foreign man stand over it.

There's a light stream of blood running from its nose. The man says:

"Il est mort d'hemoragie, le pauvre."

The cat was tossed from a fifth floor window, the woman tells me in Turkish. We push the cat closer to the thick, high wall behind Galatasaray High School; by now it's clearly dead. The woman on the fifth floor throws coal into her stove. The weather's so cold. If only it would snow. Even when it snows, there's some warmth in the air.

When did Panco get back from Alemdağ? Here he is, walking past me. He's with a friend. He acts as if he's sidestepping a dead cat. Our arms graze against each other. Walls open. People hold grudges for years, but if they both feel the same way, they kiss and make up and say enough is enough. I turn around. Panco is still walking down the street with his friend, laughing. The pool of the Munir Pasha Konak was reduced to ash but the slimy green water is still there. You can't see the bottom, but when I close my eyes now I can see the glimmering ten lira coins. Once we gave our friend, the future governor, fifty *kuruş* to jump into the pool with his clothes on.

Panco took his friend to a coffeehouse I'd never heard of. It was on the first floor of a building at the back of a little courtyard, this coffeehouse. Beside the front door was a little shop selling aluminum pots and plastic cups. When I saw them stepping through that door, curiosity got the better of me. I walked in behind them. I looked up, and there was a glass door in front of me. Beyond it was a large room filled with people playing backgammon and cards. There was a pool table in the far corner. Everyone looked up when I walked in. It must have been the sort of place with a regular crowd, because each and every one took a long look at me. No question of sitting down and ordering a coffee – it would be living hell. So I pretended to be looking for someone. Our friend Luka was there, at least. He was a mason, a painter. I could ask after him. He wore glasses. He was a Greek citizen, but really he was Albanian. I'd ask the owner about him. Then I saw Panco shielding Luka, with his own face averted. Then he looked right at me as if I were someone he was expecting, someone from long ago. He attempted a smile. Curse you, you cuckold. I turned around, but before I left, I glanced over my shoulder. Again, I could see his overcoat's fur collar.

I felt better when I saw the fur. I cast my mind back to the rabbit, the partridge, and that warm and beautiful, wondrously slippery serpent. And the blackbird. And Alemdağ. And the waters of Taşdelen, and the rotting leaves, and the white sun hanging over them, quivering like jelly.

Dolapdere

· · ·

Surely you've heard some of the names Istanbul has given its neighbor-hoods? I can't praise them enough. They're sublime, truly sublime. Pre-posterous some might be, and misleading too, but, oh, the images they conjure up! Memories come flooding in so fast I begin to wonder if it's a film I'm watching, here in the darkness of my mind.

Before you even shut your eyes, you see a mill churning water in the orchards of Dolapdere, and in each orchard, a well with an enormous bucket and an old workhorse with a scarf wrapped around his eyes; you hear squeaking as water drips from the bottom of a bucket; you hear clat-tering chains, as the mill horse's muscles twitch and sunlight dances in the water flowing through the wooden runnels. The workhorse pauses, then picks up speed as a gardener cries out in surprise, and then we see the bright pink heels of a barefoot Albanian girl, and cucumber flowers in a coiled red moustache, and swirling cigarette smoke as an angry gardener in his fifties lights up; and a brazen bitch with a dark nose and a dark mouth and a wet tongue that is a shade of pink we rarely see anymore – but we see the fur on her back in hackles, and her tail circling angrily in the air . . .

You can reach this neighborhood from anywhere in Beyoğlu and go as far as the bus station, but I took the most enchanting route of all: I walked down through Elmadağ.

Elmadağ is on a steep hill. Its houses stand upright in neat rows. Strolling down through this neighborhood you will find neither apples nor mountains – just a pavement long since crumbled. Now you're in a poor neighborhood. You see little makeshift houses of wood, stone, sheet iron, and cardboard. You see naked children and coffeehouses stripped bare – no mirrors here, or straw, or chairs. People mill about in the neighborhood square and their accents tell you where they're from. Someone says:

"Brother, ain't your girl in the factory?"

Another:

"Hey there, Rüstem, they fire your olive-skinned girl again? She'll be out on the street selling trinkets."

This neighborhood is as noisy as a festival – everywhere you can hear drums, wooden horns and fiddles. Old men sporting dark moustaches and thin trousers wander the streets, and their women make your heart jump with their pungent scent. In the mud you can see the tracks from last winter (no not last winter, a winter long before that) and horseshoe prints unwashed by the rains that fell the day after Mehmet the Conqueror took Constantinople. There's a sharp reek of ammonia along the base of the wall. It stings your eyes as you continue down the hill, past a printing factory that is busy churning. Most of the young men in the neighborhood work there. The miserable unpaved streets surrounding it stink of pulp, ammonia and Moroccan leather. This is Watermill. When you're back on the asphalt you can walk on to Yenişehir. Aghia Vangelistra looms like a feudal castle on the right, and in the evening, on saint's days, the great church is alight with candles and chandeliers, and when you look inside you half expect to see counts and dukes in powdered white wigs dancing the polka with princesses in low-cut gowns.

Hundreds of Christian girls from here come of age in Beyoğlu, toiling away in all the shops: tailors, barbershops, nightclubs, clothing shops, patisseries, bars, seamstresses, furriers and cinemas; their brothers become the city's masons, painters, jeweler apprentices, lathe men, button salesmen, carpenters, joiners, and master locksmiths. Maids and servants begin life here, too.

You run into all sorts in this neighborhood: remorseful pickpockets; heroin addicts just out of the hospital; fortune-tellers; Balkan immigrants from 1900 and 1953; old-world thespians; handsome young toughs with bob knives; petty crooks, con men and gigolos; mothers pimping daughters and husbands seeking customers for their wives; the smell of lamb cutlets, hunger, rakı, love, lust, good, evil, and the opposite of every word.

When night falls you hear whispering on the dark corners, and on every street, sweet nothings in Greek . . .

When it rains, it floods here first, and when other neighborhoods in Istanbul are steeped in the cool dreams of an evening summer wind, the leaves on the trees in this neighborhood are still. The coffeehouses and tavernas of Yenişehir are big and beautiful and the square is drenched in light and the smell of roasted intestines, fried mussels, oysters, scallops, red radishes, parsley, fried liver, wine, fish entrails and rakı. Here you see outrageously passionate men in their fifties wearing bell bottoms, pointy shoes and red sashes. Their hair is stuck to their foreheads, and their only forays outside the neighborhood have been to prison.

Yani Usta

. . .

He must have been fifteen when I met him. He wasn't Yani Usta yet – he was just a boy. A dark-skinned boy with dark hair, dark eyes, dark legs.

And me? Well I was a grown man. Why should I lie – I had no money, no job. I didn't know a soul in the world. There was only my mother. I had no one else. Yani Usta's twenty now, and I'm pushing fifty. But he's my only real friend. The way he can splash those walls with oil paint! It's amazing, just amazing. But to me he's still that dark-skinned boy. He'd put his brush down, and he'd be gone. Sometimes it was a football match, sometimes a movie. Sometimes it was a coffeehouse for a game of hearts.

If I happened to flitter through his mind, he'd come and find me. If I didn't, he wouldn't bother.

"Why look for you, Granddad?" he'd say.

We had this quiet beer hall. A place where I would go and sit. And think, and think. What have I done for this world? What have I seen? Why am I here? Why do I have to leave at all? What have I done?

It's warm in here, but I still feel the chill from the snow outside. It's six o'clock and the place is still empty. The waiter has gone into the other room. The clock on that wall can make a man nervous, and drive him to drink.

Should I wait for Yani Usta? He won't come if I wait . . . And will he come if I don't? There's hope. There's hope when I'm not waiting.

He'll come and sit down across from me. What will I say to him? What will he say to me? I can never remember. Later I'll make something up. He says this, he says that.

There are regulars here at the beer hall. There's this one fellow who comes and sits by the window. He opens a bottle of soda. He pours in a double shot of rakı, and then a single shot. He orders a plate of dried fruit, a plate of grilled kidney, and maybe an omelet.

Yani Usta comes in. His forehead is in knots. The girl's dad is giving him five thousand lira drachmas. They say she's pretty enough. He knew her already but this time he was at their place for tea. "Why don't you dance with her, Yani!" the girl's mother says. "I can't dance for the life of me," Yani Usta said, "and even if I did, you can be sure I wouldn't dance right now!" The woman still wanted to close the deal. "Talk to my dad," Yani Usta said.

So it looks like Yani Usta won't be coming here anymore to share a beer or two. "I shouldn't be seen in these kinds of places for a while," he says. "There's five thousand lira riding on this."

"Oh, Yani," I say. "Those were the days! Just the other night you were a scrawny little dark-skinned boy. Now you're all grown up. And I'm the granddad. The beer hall is the old beer hall. The tables the old tables. The world a different world. But you're a different man. And I'm still the same old granddad. Yani Usta! I'll always see you like you were way back when: a dark-haired, dark-eyed little devil. Remember how we'd go to the movies together? How you'd go wild sitting next to me – clap your hands, slap me on the back?

"*Viresi*," you'd say, "did you see that? Check out that spy. See what he did? With just one punch . . ."

That movie theater's gone now, too. The one with all the mirrors. On rainy days, it stank of people and clothes. There in the first-class section, surrounded by all those boys, my heart would almost burst with love; every face was beautiful; every boy was kind; every hand was small, dirty, warm, and calloused.

Days went by and things took a turn for the worse. The drink was taking its toll. You grew up, enough to take those five thousand lira drachmas. Do you at least love the girl, Yani Usta?

"She's a woman, isn't she, Granddad? How could I not?"

"That's right, Yani Usta. Women should be loved, it's only natural, I suppose, but I love children more than women because I've always been a child at heart."

"Don't you love me?"

"You? How could you ask such a thing, Yani Usta? You? I love you very much."

"But I'm no longer a child."

"You are to me."

"If you still thought of me as a boy I'd never forgive you. I'd never let it go. I'd never speak to you again, ever."

"You'll invite me to the wedding, Yani Usta?"

"What is it with you? Of course I will."

For a moment we are silent. Then he asks me something and I'm not sure why:

"You go to theaters and stuff like that, don't you? Bring me along one evening."

"Sure, whenever you want," I say.

We agree on Monday night. I go to the sales window early and buy the tickets and leave. When I get back Yani Usta is waiting for me, all dressed up. He's come all right but the tickets are for the following night. There are no performances on Monday.

"Yani Usta, there aren't ever plays on Mondays. These tickets are for tomorrow night," I say.

"Never mind, just give me my ticket," he says.

We drink four beers each and then we go our separate ways. The next night I am at the theater at eight. He still isn't there. The bell rings. The curtains close. Someone comes in and sits beside me.

Yani Usta isn't coming; he's sold his ticket.

He's pulled one last childish trick on me. And it's a good one. But how strange I feel, how lonely. I'm always going to the theater alone, and usually it's fine. I like it best when I'm sitting on the upper balcony, and the theater is almost empty. Tonight's performance is probably the worst I've ever seen.

So what's up, Yani Usta? Where were you tonight? If you didn't show, well, you didn't show. So what? When I see you in the street, you're still that little boy beside me in that movie theater with all the mirrors. That doesn't mean I can't feel something like a steel fist, wrenching my heart. But enough about that! Don't take it so seriously. It's nothing! Don't get upset. Forget it, Yani Usta! Just flash me a smile when you see me. Don't get upset – that's the last thing I wanted. What's a night at the theater any-way? Nothing, damn it! Not when there's friendship in the world. That's one thing that hasn't died.

Death of the Dülger

. . .

They all have beautiful eyes, and when they're still alive you might imagine their scales on a woman's dress, or pinned to her breast, or dangling from her ears. Forget diamonds. Forget rubies, emeralds, and carnelians. There isn't a gemstone in this world that can outshine these scales.

If they could, women would waltz into ballrooms flashing this living iridescence; fishermen would be millionaires and fish would have all the glory and fame. But the moment a fish dies its scales go dull, until it's as gray as an old doll. Unless, like the fish in this story, it had had no burning, shimmering scales to lose. The poor thing had no scales at all. The Dülger is olive brown with a light, faint touch of green. It's the ugliest fish in the sea, with an enormous, toothless mouth that glistens translucent white, like nylon. It spreads open wide the moment it surfaces; and once its mouth opens it never closes again.

Did I say that it's a dirty olive brown? And as flat as a pancake? Did I say it has two dark spots on either side that look like fingerprints?

Once upon a time the Dülger was a terrible sea monster: it wreaked havoc on the Mediterranean long before the birth of Jesus Christ. After which the Greek fishermen began calling him *Hrisopsaros*, Christ's Fish. Woe to the Likyan who slipped overboard. Who knows how many Carthaginians the Dülger dragged into the sea, how many Jews it tossed up into the air? It sliced them and diced them and chopped them into bits; it threw them in the air and poked them and stabbed them. It pummeled and battered them and tore them into pieces. The Dülger was the most fearsome creature in the Mediterranean, and pirates, undaunted by man, beast, lightning, rain, misfortune or torture, turned white upon hearing its name.

One day Jesus was strolling along the seashore when he saw a group of fishermen abandoning their boats. He could see that terror had gripped them. "What's the matter?" he asked. "Oh Lord," they cried. "We've had enough! Enough of this monster! It's dashed our boats and ripped our people to shreds. And the worst of it is that we no longer dare go out to fish. We are doomed to go hungry and die."

In his humble robe, Jesus stepped toward the sea that was the raging Dülger's domain. Pinning the largest between his long fingers, he pulled it up out of the water, and, pinching it tightly, he bent over and whispered something into its ear.

And from that day on, the Dülger has been a meek and rather miserable creature, its frightful appearance notwithstanding. For the Dülger is covered in protrusions that might be mistaken for nails or files, or chisels, adzes and saws. There are even bulges that resemble pincers, and there are thorns of all sizes between its bones. Surely this is how the Dülger came to be called the woodworker fish in Turkish.

Its motley collection of tools is covered by that membrane you might take for clear nylon. It is paper-thin and gets a little thicker, a little darker, toward the tail, which is much like that of any other fish.

The instant a Dülger bites your line, it's at war with the world and the sea. We can only imagine its fear. It has already left its world behind. Even if it breaks free from the line, it'll just lie there flat on the water's surface, its wide eyes staring mournfully. Then you'll pull it up into the boat and for many minutes you'll listen to it wail. Oh, that moan. Only the Dülger and the Red Gurnard give out this pained cry. As they lie dying on the boat, they wail and gasp. When a net falls over a Dülger, it is fury incarnate.

One day in front of the fishermen's coffeehouse, I saw a Dülger hanging from an acacia tree newly blooming with white and red blossoms. It was dark brown, as if it had just come out of the sea. And it seemed entirely still, as lifeless as a stone. But I thought I caught its paper-thin membrane quivering over all those tools, as soft as silk. I'd never seen such a dance, yes, that's what it was, a dance: it was the dance of an invisible inner breath. But the body was lifeless, utterly lifeless: only the membrane was trembling, shivering with pleasure and delight. This was a dance of death. It was as if its soul was leaving its body in little breaths, slipping through its paper-thin membrane, leaving not so much as a whisper behind.

You know the way a ripple will cross the surface of the water on still summer days. That was how it looked to me. But the fish was dying, so perhaps these were tremors of pain. Perhaps we would prefer not to know. It was, after all, an extraordinary way to die. Did the fish believe it was still underwater, swimming happily along the sea floor? Night had fallen. It could feel the sand tickling him. The eggs were there and the male seeds were swaying in the waters above, or so it thought. It was seized by a moment of lust. Then, to my horror, it slowly began to fade, casting off its color, turning ghostly pale. Or did it just seem that way? Was it really changing color? No need for me to take a closer look – I knew I was right.

The edges of its membrane along its sides began to quicken the dance and from one second to the next turned even paler. I could sense the fear in its heart, a fear that we all know: the fear of dying.

Now it knew. Its life at the bottom of the sea was no longer. Its flat body would never again drift through the currents, or bury itself in dark waters and green seaweed. It would no longer wake in a cool light showering down from the surface, or splash its tail about in the dance of green and blue daylight, casting off its seeds before racing to the surface. No more dozing in the iridescent seaweed, no more rubbing that set of tools against barnacles for a good cleaning. It was all over.

The Dülger took a long time dying. It was as if it were trying to accustom itself to the collection of gases we know as air. If it could have just held out a little longer, it might have made it.

If only we could have just drawn out its death throes from two hours to four, and then from four to eight, and from eight to twenty-four. If we'd managed that, we might even see a Dülger working among us one fine day.

And what a celebration we'll have, the day he can at last breathe our air and drink our water. We shall see at last that, despite his gross and gruesome looks, he is actually quite a calm and timid creature, sensitive and good-hearted by nature, with a soft and hesitant demeanor. He'll become one of us. We'll praise him and do our best to make him happy. He'll find it all a little strange at first, but he'll do his best to fit in. Then one day we'll turn him into a frustrated, misunderstood poet. And the next day we'll slander him and run him into the ground. The day after we'll harangue him for being too sensitive. The day after that, we'll harangue him for loving us, and on the last day we'll accuse him of his cowardice and silence. One by one, we'll pull out all the beautiful things inside him and toss them aside. We'll sneer as we chip away at those two fingerprints with his ax, his saw, his file, his adze, and nails. And he'll become the monster that he was at the dawn of time.

Once we get him hooked on our water, we'll leap at the chance to change him back into a monster.

I Can't Go into Town

. . .

I seem to be starting another story. But it's been months since I picked up a pen. As if I might actually come up with something. I doubt it. But that's fine. Truth is I'm happy with the way things are. So what's come over me tonight? What made me sit down to scribble out these lines? If I really put my mind to it, I could come up with a good lie. I could claim to be driven by some mysterious force. But that's not it. It's always like this. I can dash out a story while I wait for a ferry, balancing on one foot.

Don't take this the wrong way, now. I'm not pretending someone just asked me how I write. That I could never pin down. I'm just taking a closer look at the evening. Now I'll admit that it was a dark mood that brought me to this sheet of yellow paper that I picked up at the corner store. What I'm trying to understand is why one dark mood leads me to an even darker one, when there are so many other things I could do to chase it away.

That's just how it is. But why? I have all these books to read. I don't have much money, but I have a home. I have a wood-burning stove and food. There's a radio downstairs . . . I can't go into town. I just can't go, but you're not to think I don't have it in me to climb a mountain. Ha! I'd throw on my cap and it's high-ho to Kalpazankaya. The sun's nearly setting. Oh God, watch out! "The sun's nearly setting." Now for a description of the world. But my heart's just not in it: no painting the waves for me tonight, no toasting the horizon like a slice of bread.

See! We did it again. We painted the waves. We toasted the horizon just perfectly.

That's just how we are. We were trained to write bad literature: there's no way around it. We should turn back to poetry.

I said I couldn't go into town. Why not? So here's the crux of the matter. Over the last four or five lines I've been holding back a secret. Something really strange. The key is in the sentence, I can't go into town. I can't tell you how much I'd like to unravel it for you. But it's not in my power. No really, it's there. I just can't write it down. Wouldn't they laugh at me if I did? But what's wrong with that? If man wasn't born to be ridiculed, then he was born to laugh at others. It all leads to the same door. Or it leads nowhere. They're one and the same. But I can. I hate to see someone laughed at. Do I like to be laughed at? Who would? That goes without saying. Well then you'll say, look, you're making a distinction. But if I were to say I did this to feel more human, you couldn't say I was soft in the head. And if you did, then the hell with it! All men are flawed, all animals, too . . .

What if I told you I was a civil servant, and relatively well-off? Earning as much as four or five hundred lira a month. With two daughters. Who are at the school just over there. With a confident, well-dressed woman for a wife. I bring home all the money I earn. My main monthly expense is a kilo of rakı. We have a refrigerator at home, I don't know how it got there, but it's there. I keep the bottles inside. Sometimes, at the beginning of the month, I still have one bottle with two fingers left in it. I hold myself back so I can share a little with a friend who swings by in the evening. No matter what state he's in! Let's say I have other bad habits. I have a few running tabs here and there. To be paid at the top of the month, of course. There's a debt of sixty-three lira and eighty-five *kuruş* that I'll need to wriggle away from the wife. Maybe I spent it all carousing. Maybe it's just a small tab at the tobacconist, for newspapers and Bafra cigarettes; two or three beers and a lemon soda at the club; and almost seventeen lira at the patisserie.

How can I go into town when I still haven't paid off last month's debts, when I also need fifty-six lira for other inevitable expenses? I can't show my face down there, can I? I could end the story just like that. Some would laugh. Others would pity me. Some would say, "Now there's a real story."

Some would be delighted and say, "He can't write any more." But then you all know that I'm not a civil servant. A civil servant might be the type to get hung up on the shopkeeper or the street sweeper, or tobacconist – schmabacconist! Or maybe not. He might not. If he did, he wouldn't owe more than three packs of Bafra, three cones from the ice-cream man, no more than seven coffees from the coffee house. Ipso facto, I wouldn't care if I did.

That's not why I can't go into town. Well then, why can't I? Are you even interested? I doubt it. You couldn't care less, I'm sure. If you think I'm making too big a deal of this, go ahead and say so. But it's not being able to go downtown that gave me the key to this story. If I tried to explain why, though . . . it would take me too long. So why waste more time? Let's just say I can't bear seeing anyone and end it there.

Enough of this! From now on: I just can't go into town, and that's that.

Oh, these prohibitions! These prohibitions that we place on ourselves. And the ones that others place on us and we place on them. That the state places on its citizens, and the citizens on the state, and municipalities on residents, and residents on the municipality . . .

If we can't live in a world of prohibitions, then how can we live in a world without them? Why is it that animals, even our pets, can live quite happily without them? They lead simple lives, bounding here and there, feeling oh so fine, apart from the racket they kick up when they need to kill their hunger – while we seem to believe that we can't survive, unless we're hemmed in by laws. We might even describe humans as animals who are against the law. Isn't each and every germ against the law? Love is against the law, too. The day will come when water and food will be, too. We'll each be out of bounds for all others.

I can't kiss that beautiful boy when I want to! I can't swim in the sea when I want to; my lungs are weak and the doctor has forbidden it. I can't drink when I want to; it's come to the point where I'm afraid, it strangles my mind, my liver forbids it. I can't just hop onto a boat for Haydarpaşa and huff it all the way out to Van. I'd croak along the way . . . I can't go into town. God damn the place anyway. The shopkeeper from Karaman might very well have pearls threaded into his moustache and he may have gilded his hair in gold. He might have encased his entire body in silver. But then what's silver to him?

And the delicatessen – that man has stocked his place so full of food that even if he took all his sausages to the pier, and got a fire going, and invited the whole town to get their fill of sausage and wine, while the cats swarmed, and the dogs howled, and the torches flamed, even if he banded together with all the fishermen and Kurdish porters and cats and dogs of all the summer houses of Istanbul to put on a wedding party lasting forty days and forty nights, only then would he run out of supplies. And if on the forty-first day he got in more salami and sausages, and fresh cheese and wine, he'd have enough to enrich himself for another forty days.

He'd still wander around town in his disgusting apron, sucking on the fenugreek seeds in his teeth. That dark moustache would still glisten with oil, and his skin would still stink of garlic. His stomach would still be sprinkled with cheese crumbs, and his wrists would be as thick as my ankles.

And then – the baker! That bullwhip of a baker who flogs his oil-drenched pastry off on the child laborers in the morning for thirty-five *kuruş*. That's all very well, but he never gives you change and you're always too scared to ask for it because he'll just give you more bread instead. He's always having new houses built so he can rent them out. He lets his goats gobble through the freshest shrubbery in the village . . .

And then there's the master butcher you can smell from fifty feet away, who sits in his chair from morning till night, dreaming of goats and buffaloes and fatty organs, who pads that nasty organ fat into every half kilo of meat he puts through his grinder. You might think I don't want to go into town because I don't want to look these people in the eye. But that's not it, not at all, that's not why I won't go into town, because be sure that if I did, I'd call out to the shopkeeper, "Hey Barba Niko," and to the baker, "Oho, master Haralambo," and to the butcher, "Oooooh, Abdülbekir."

It's not like they're the only ones in town. There's Iskanavi, the proprietor of our coffeehouse. A man without a care in the world. He doesn't even know the meaning of money. He's just a little more distracted when he doesn't have it, like anyone else. And when he has it, he's always laughing. For him, a ten-lira note and a hundred-lira note are more or less the same thing. He doesn't ask for much. He's a sweet man. During one of the wars, he hid in the attic until it was over. He only came out to the square when the armistice was announced. He had all kinds of stories about his days up in the attic.

What hardship! During the war he had to rent out his home for the summer. His wife would stare up at the ceiling for hours, marveling at how her husband could live up there without ever making a sound. One day he was driven almost insane by the sound of people dancing the Hasapiko. Another day the tenants were astounded to see a knife from a hole in the ceiling plunge into a chunk of cheese sitting on the dinner table, only to float back up to the attic, right before their very eyes. Once they learned how it got up there, and why, and that the author of this act had done so while perfectly sane, they began to have him down for dinner every night.

He was a crafty little fellow.

And then there's barber Hilmi, with his sparkling eyes and his shiny bald pate – if he starts on his sensational tales from his youth, just watch out. He'll leave you rolling on the floor. Oh, the tricks this handsome barber played on his lovers. Always a happy ending, but so many twists and turns along the way. He has such a light touch. How gracefully he weaves in the guile and the subterfuge, how much sweeter life was then, and how playful.

Who else? There's Pandeli Efendi the milkman. He used to keep an old pistol hanging in his shop. People who came in after six were members of the club. The Firing Club. Blasts of all kinds were fair game.

Now this may seem a little unsavory, but the truth is if a member didn't fire one off from the mouth (or some other orifice) the exact moment he stepped in through the door, he was out of the game. But if he did, Pandeli Efendi would push aside the heavy, old veteran cooks and gardeners and greengrocers and put him at the head of the table. Nobody ever laughed. But it was there in our eyes, unless, of course, the shot had overwhelmed us. And slowly it would fade and the discussion would turn to the news of the day and the foolishness of those who make money only to squirrel it away. Having passed a motion to the effect that people like this are never satisfied until they die, the meeting would adjourn.

Why won't I go into town then? I'm a member of the club. I could listen to a world of stories for the price of a haircut. I'd split my sides laughing. Or I could swing by Iskanvi Efendi's coffeehouse.

"So, Iskanavi Efendi," I'd say. "What happened when the old woman saw that piece of cheese floating up to the ceiling?"

"She made a cross on her chest and said *'Panaya mou.'* Then, *'Viresi'* and *'Calliope'* and *'Ti pzagma, tinatnoyni.'*"

"But why the hell did you expose yourself like that?"

"I got tired of it all, brother. I wanted them to know that I was up there. I made so much noise up there at night, but neither the husband nor the wife ever got up. They were dead to the world. But sometimes they would get up and call to my wife. '*Viresi*,' they'd say. '*Calliope! Pondika!* It sounds like there's a rat as big as a man up there!' And I was worried that they'd talk about it and the whole thing would get out of hand. So that was my way of telling them that there weren't rats in the attic."

So there you go. The town is *haram*, it's sinful. I can imagine it now, all those little twenty-five watt bulbs glowing, and all the flies. I want to explain why – why I can't go downtown. But what use would that be? Who'd care?

I put on my hat and my fisherman's jacket and I wrapped a scarf around my head like I had a toothache. I went out and walked past the coffeehouse. He was there, he was there.

I came back home. I got into bed and turned off the light. I thought for a while. I thought about killing anyone who said I couldn't go into town, no matter who it was. It was the first time I'd ever had a thought like that.

I got dressed again and went back out. I went straight to the coffee-house. I walked to the far end and sat down. His face went bright yellow when he saw me. His lips were trembling. In the coffeehouse mirror I saw the white, jaundiced face of a man. I flinched – it was me. I got out of there fast.

"Iskanavi," I said, "I'll have a coffee. Now about that attic story . . ."

He was broke and in a bad mood.

"You've got nothing to worry about," he said. "Your salt is dry. But mine – δεν είναι, no."

．　．　．

I could finish the story like that. It would be one of my classic endings. It could be, but no. I don't go into town, I don't go into that bright white coffeehouse. I don't sit down opposite someone who doesn't want to see me, and I don't say a word to the proprietor.

I'm at home, in my room. I can't go into town. I have a fever of thirty-nine degrees. I'm cold and trembling. Sometimes I'm on fire. My mother rubs vinegar on my temples. No more reading, she says. It's time to sleep. She turns off the light and leaves. I listen to the sounds around me. The dogs on Spoon Island are still barking. The wind is pounding the window-panes, rattling the doors. I switch on the light . . .

Well that would be another kind of ending, but this isn't it either. No, this isn't the one either. I can't go into town, and that's that.

The Boy on the Tünel

Nothing is too much for these people.

· · ·

Lately I've been spending my nights in a very strange neighborhood. There's this black haze that rises from the sea around nine o'clock. It spreads and spreads, until it has enveloped us all. As the neighborhood sleeps, a cool breeze wafts through it, seeking human company, but settling down with the stray dogs and the lonely cats in the dark, quiet streets. Until the new day dawns, that's all there is.

Once there was a Greek entrepreneur who ran two dynamos on diesel. This was the only source of electricity; a yellow, morbid *courant continu* that turned us all into ghostly and indecipherable blurs. Now the municipality and the entrepreneur have had a disagreement and the lights are out. Who knows where these dark streets might take you after half past eight?

As for the residents – those who are fond of their wives stay at home all night, smoking at their windowsills, planning the next day's arguments.

In the distance you only see the torches made of rags dipped in any gasoline they could lay their hands on. The flames slash through the darkness. Staring out over this haunted landscape, they catch glimpses of the houses along the coast. They track the lights and the sounds; they drift off into a trance that is not quite sleep; they see the crabs.

I spoke about these long, dark nights with a Turkish lady who went to a private lycée (a lady, no less, who speaks both English and French!) and she said:

"Even the people there are too dark!"

Thick mustachioed Greek fishermen, scrawny bare-legged children, Kurdish porters whose windpipes are bursting from their throats, ninety-year-old Greek women, the postman and the delivery boy at the corner shop. They can all count themselves among those people, and so can you and I.

So there I was, conversing with this woman. Someone else was standing a little further on. The greengrocer was in his corner, and the delivery boy was halfway up the hill, beautiful and forlorn.

I didn't disagree with her. What would be the point! She is on casual terms with the head of the neighborhood. She gives men ideas, and women advice.

I went into Istanbul that day. And I am writing this description of a boy on the Tünel for the boy on the Tünel, not for this woman – I have long since given up on her.

We entered the Tünel in Beyoğlu. There weren't many people traveling down the hill just then. We were in the second-class car. There were three soldiers in a corner, a woman of a certain age with her daughter-in-law, and further on there was a noisy Armenian group on their way to catch a boat, and the boy, and me.

He had tucked his bare feet beneath the seat as far back as he could. You wouldn't have noticed them unless you had been paying close attention. The train hadn't started moving. The gate dividing the first and second-class cars and the gate to the platform kept opening and closing.

Then they closed with a sigh like the breath of a fish pulled from the sea.

His fingers were curled under his ear lobe and his mouth hung open. His other hand was on his knee; it was filthy and black, but despite the dark olive color of his skin his nails were pure white. His fingers were long and slender. The patterns on his shirt were like oil paint and so pale they were almost white.

He wore a mother-of-pearl hook fastened tightly around his thin, grimy neck. Now for his face . . .

His nose was flat, his mouth wide open and salivating. His large, dark brown eyes were brimming with an innocence that was almost inhuman; they were literally white with astonishment. His hair was a mess, and flecked with cigarette ash.

When the doors closed – I was standing right beside him – he lifted up his head to look at me. I had already assumed my position. I was looking elsewhere, with grave contemplation. First he lowered his eyes, and then his face. Then I started watching him again. The smile on his face was so faint and so true; how it lit up his lips, his eyes, his eyebrows . . .

Oh, to see the joy of this ride in the face of a twelve-year-old boy! Maybe I was that happy my first time, too. We see such joy in children all the time. They clap their hands and cry:

"Look, father! Look how wonderful it is!"

Nothing could stop us showing the joy we felt.

But this boy on the Tünel – he is trying not to show it. Rattling and shaking, we rumble down the hill. Now he is watching the lady standing with her young daughter just across from him. They aren't even looking at him. He seems to relax a bit. Again he looks up at me. I pretend to be deep in my newspaper. He relaxes even more. But then he senses something; he feels my eyes on him, and other eyes, too; and the light and the diabolical slamming of the wheels against the tracks. He can no longer take pleasure in this. There's that little smile again; that tiny, fearful, forlorn burst of innocence. Now from a distance we watch the slow and heavy opening of the hemisphere of the door on the Galata side of the Tünel line; he is watching and so am I. The little smile is still fixed on his face. Now we're on the other side. The little boy's face is glistening like a freshly peeled almond. A bright streak passes across his dark, dark face. It could be a waterfall, it could be a torch. It washes him clean as it bathes him in light. But it passes too quickly for me to see it. The flame flickers, and then there is that sad little smile again. This time he catches me. He catches me watching him. The smile vanishes. I have smothered him with the tired fears of a man who has been on the Tünel a hundred, maybe a thousand times, but still worries it might collapse on him. The doors grind open. As he races away on his long, slender legs, with his pure, white finger nails flashing, I manage to catch up with him. We are out of the Tünel now. Wandering through the evening crowd, his mouth falls open, as he marvels at the speed of his journey, as he watches the next wave of passengers, hurrying up to Beyoğlu. It is almost as if . . . yes. It is almost as if he is taking the scene into his mouth.

Elated, he races away. I watch him go. Even those wide, torn patches on his trousers look pleased. Sewn with large stitches and ripped at the bottom, they speak of the wonders they witnessed, there in that seat on the Tünel.

His black legs plunge into the crowd.

Everything about him tells you that he spends his winters in a tinplate house and his summers in a tent.

We built these funiculars for people, so that they could get to the top of a hill in a single moment. But for a child who doesn't want to show the joy he feels when he rides it for the first time, the Tünel is also a slide.

I won't be so bold as to say that if we can't make our funiculars as slides, it's because we don't appreciate the children who feel such joy on their first ride down. That would be flattering myself. That would be assuming I had the power to build such a slide myself! Let them come to me with their tenders! But what I will say is this:

"Nothing is too much for these people."

Tonight in Edirnekapı a mother will listen to the story of a boy riding the Tünel. "Then this man with these enormous eyes started staring at me," he'll say. "And after that I just couldn't enjoy myself." He'll tell his mother how he just couldn't find it in himself to smile at those strangers. Let alone show them his white teeth. He'll tell her what he heard along the way, and what he couldn't say, and they will be as happy as if they had just taken a ride on the Tünel.

His Uncle's Coat

. . .

Born in 1921, Mehmet Dalgır was a big, blundering man whose forelock only half concealed a narrow forehead. His mouth hung open. His shirt was ripped open, and his skin was dark, almost purple. His eyes were vacant, drained of everything but dread.

"Can't you see, Mr. Judge? I'm trembling like a leaf."

His face went into spasms as his left arm twitched.

"You see, my head's not in the right place . . ."

"Where's your head?"

"On my shoulders."

"And your mind?"

"It's just not there. I lost it. I even spent some time in the loony bin. But if I get off, I'm sure to get a job. I'm a carpenter, you see. And I know all the tricks. Why would I lie? I know them all. Forgive me and I won't do it again. I'll go straight to a carpenter and . . . I'll take whatever he's willing to pay me for the week. Just to make ends meet."

"It seems like your mind's all there, Mehmet."

"It comes and goes, sir."

"Do you have a criminal record?"

"I do, sir. There was that time I took my uncle's coat. That's why all this happened. I stole those clothes so I could pay him back. Oh, that coat! That's what got me into all this trouble in the first place. That coat's the one to blame."

"Were you given a sentence?"

"I was. A month in jail, but I haven't done the time yet, honored sir."

Now his trousers were trembling. So, too, was his shirt, whose reverse side was as purple as a bruise, and the ripped rubber around his feet.

In that moment of silence, I looked at Mehmet Dalgır's profile: his mouth was ajar, and on his chin was a straggle of black stubble: half a face and half a mind. A frightened child: half calculating and half pleading.

"My mind's not all there."

"Well then, just tell me what happened."

"Around eight I went into a garden in Vefa. I went up one, two, three steps, then I slipped through a half-open door of the house. The clothes were there on a shelf. I took everything, and I hid them in the Şehzade Mosque."

"What did you take?"

"A coat, a silk shirt, a little pillow, two felt hats, a cap, a pair of shoes, and two woolen undershirts, which I put on right away. They took them from me though, at the police station. They took everything I had. But I haven't said what happened the day before that. What happened was, an *eskici* passed by. *Give me your old clothes! Give me your old clothes!* That's what he kept saying, but when I did, they pounced on us, took us both off to the station. And they kept me in for three days. The other bastard got away, but not with the clothes. They returned them to their rightful owners, even the woolen undershirt. It's not on me now. You can see that, can't you?"

"Why did you spend three days in the station? Maybe you didn't tell them the truth?"

"I did. I mean . . . I told them everything I'm telling you now."

Mehmet looked at the judge in disbelief as he tapped out everything they had said on a typewriter. A little later I even saw him nodding approvingly. He was beaming like a happy child, thrilled by the idea of a judge committing his words to paper. His left arm was still twitching. His thick, fat lower lip kept moving, as if he were reading something and mouthing the words.

"I won't do it again. I swear I won't do it again. I only did it to buy my uncle's coat. That's what I told myself, you see. I said, 'I can get his coat back if I sell these things, and then I'll get out of jail.' My uncle was hopping mad. He wouldn't even let me in the house . . ."

The judge tapped it all down. "I did the job to pay for my uncle's coat."

Mehmet Dalgır:

"Yeah, that's it. If I did the job, well, that's why I did it. For my uncle's coat . . . And if I get off I'll go straight out and find a carpenter . . ."

Mehmet didn't get off. Given the nature of the crime and the absence of proof, the court's official decision was that Mehmet Dalgır would be detained in a police station cell until a date was set for determining his sentence.

When he was outside, Mehmet Dalgır asked the police officer next to him:

"What happened?"

"You're going to jail until the court comes to a decision."

"Do they have any positions there?"

"Sure."

"Do they teach carpentry?"

"Of course," the officer said.

His left arm was twitching, his lower lip, too.

Kalinikta

. . .

When I looked up, I was alone, but a moment ago people were all around me, there were geese and dogs and trees rustling the air. A stream was bubbling in my ear, as trees washed its waters, animals were embracing men and men animals. Dogs spoke and humans howled. In a yellow sky someone cried:

"You are my soul, my tree, my stream, my sea." And the other was warm inside his human smell. There was no answer. But friendship coursed through his dark blue veins and into the sea; his hair was dark; his eyes, too, and his brow. He was brimming with dark days and dark stories; the love songs he would sing later were already on his lips.

Was the moon rising above the sun from inside our little boat? Or was it rising up from the dust, up in the sky or the trees' red edges? I had one lip pressed down. The other moved in and out of me like the fire on its tail.

"I feel your pulse in my veins. I hear it surging through my wrists . . ."

Trees are flirting with the stars that shimmer like candles on their boughs. My most steadfast friends are here: sakız rakı in my glass, my tongue beating the rhythm of a stutter, a fishing rod in my hand, a hook at its end, Barba Stanco in the boat, the bow pointed toward Sivriada and all the stars in my breast. I am at the rudder. The motor is churning the sea. Churning and churning. The dogs are barking in welcome; the trees draw in the stars, then the hills, as the baying dogs usher in the morning. I drink in the smell of fish, the smell of fried mussels from a Greek house on the shore; my moustache still holds the smell of anisette.

"You are my soul," I say.

I breathe in the smell of stars fallen into my cup; they smell of rich coffee. The arbutus flowers have crumbled. I crush French lavender in the palm of my hand. Bees land on my tongue and sting my eyes. The sun is setting and a cormorant sinks into thought, a seagull alights on a pylon in the void. The pebbles on the shore wear the water's cloak and soldiers come out wearing all the colors of the sky. I hear footsteps on the pebbled shore: That's Aspasya, Jasmine Aspasya, who smells of camphor, Aspasya dressed in the yellow of Easter flowers as sparks swirl around her, and a serpent; there are mirrors and fountains on her tongue.

"You are my soul," I say, "my soul."

Yani! Hey Yani. Black Yani. Hey! It's the black-eyed barrel organ-maker from Beykoz I'm talking to now. The son of Panayot, my old friend, Yani! Sing *Black Pepper* to me in Greek, so that Aspasya might also hear. I am Ibrahim in the song – no, not Ibrahim with all his riches, I am Black Pepper.

Whose lambs are those on Friendship Pasture? Are they yours? Are they lambs? Is that lambs bleating? Sing me *Black Pepper*, Yani.

By now it's evening in Omonya Square in Athens; a man sits on a coffee-house terrace, and on the table in front of him sits an anchovy, a green olive and a glass of mastıka. It could be anyone. The smell of jellyfish wafts in from Pireaus as Socrates ambles down from the Acropolis. It's you, Yanaki!

The most steadfast of all my friends, the very last of all my friends to die. Look up at the sky as you wander the streets of Athens. The stars will guide you to the islands, the ships, the shores, to this little boat. You'll visit all the islands of the world. You'll row in all the little rowboats of the world, you'll take the glimmering phosphorescence and the moonlight rippling on the water for fish and catch them with a thirty-five centimeter nylon rod. But forget about fish for a moment and think about it, Yanakimu. Leap onto the back of a star. Look over the islands. There's only one Burgazada. That there where Leandros swam to Kaloyero, you will see one little boat. That's me: that's my boat. It's just one boat in a sea of boats, in a sea of seas. In a sea of humanity, it's just me.

Yani, it's evening in Omonya Square. Songs float out of little boats and up into the sky as light reflects off the cars. But did you hear the neighing of a horse? Did a phaeton race across your mind, or across the windows of the coffeehouses in Omonya? Do you know that I am thinking of you as I sit on this little iron fence around this little patch of grass beneath the monument in Taksim Square. I am thinking of you, Yanaki. It's evening now and the snow will soon stop falling. The electric signs are going out and the grass is growing dark. A melody with three guitars floats out from a tavern as they crush *mavrodaphne* on the streets. Don't worry about the walk back to your hotel. So what if the metro from Athens to Pireaus hasn't run for years? It's a beautiful night. You can walk, while the seagulls turn and coast in the lights above Sivriada. Barba Vasili is already in his coat and fast asleep. I'm thinking of you, Yanaki. Just this moment, the Cephalonian breeze that Apasya told us about stirs the sea around Sivriada. Yanaki, the lights in Omonya Square are going out, the coffeehouse is about to close. Have that green olive. Knock back that drink. Have you heard the foghorn on the boat from Pireaus? I am on the Galata Bridge and a tanker from Holland is sounding its horn for a fugitive crossing Okmeydan. Now I am making my way down to the dock in Üsküdar. My hands are sliding along the metal rail. Why haven't you eaten your olive? The waiter at the Ekselsiyor in Omonya Square calls out:

"*Kalinihkta*, Kiryos."

And one *kalinihkta* from me, Panco.

In the Rain

· · ·

I shouldn't have done it. But I did. I was so impolite. It wasn't anything really. But I still feel ashamed. This is how it happened:

I had drunk four or five glasses of beer. The rain outside was beyond belief. People were huddling under the eaves. But then it stopped raining quite so fiercely; the streams, rivers, and estuaries on the windowpane were gone and the muddy water running down from the top of the street was calmer and more solemn. People in a rush to get home leapt out onto the street. I suppose some of them even enjoyed being out in the rain. I suppose I must have been one of them. I was wearing a waterproof jacket. Water seeped through all the same. But never mind! I was drunk on five beers and bursting with goodwill, and I threw myself out onto the street to face the rain. I said to myself, why wait at this tram stop right in front of me. I'll walk up to the next one. The raindrops falling upon me were large and crystal clear. I could just imagine them falling on dirt roads and meadows far away. The air was rich with the smell of earth and ozone. Steam swirled up off the backs of animals. I could see villagers and barefoot, bald-headed children walking along a dirt road. A young girl suddenly leapt out from under a mulberry tree, her mouth still wet with rain. A young man behind her was holding her back.

"It's clearing, it's clearing, the clouds are breaking."

The young girl:

"We're already late . . ."

A thin river coursed down the tramway rails. The things we think of when we're drunk: how fast a piece of garbage was freewheeling down that river in the rails. Safe travels!

A drunk is a delightful fool.

I have always noticed how people are most hauntingly beautiful in thunderstorms and in the snow. You know how the farsighted blink their eyes when they try to make out people no one else would even see. They are beautiful as they struggle to see each other in the rain, and I am the object of their myopic attention . . .

I remembered a line from *The Idiot*, which I had recently read. *C'est la beauté qui sauvera le monde.*

Perhaps it's the rain that makes a person beautiful in our eyes. Perhaps it's the rain that makes us fall in love. This strange line from *The Idiot* has been knocking about in my head for days. Beauty will save the world. True in so many ways . . .

Love, violence, literature, indignity, vulgarity, elegance, good and evil, none of it will save the world. Every day we take another step toward pain and sorrow. The insight of a fool: "Beauty will save the world."

And so the role of literature on this earth: It is that thing seeking beauty. Women wear make-up to look beautiful. That man over there sports a moustache to look handsome. Will that kid keep the same face until he's fifty? He won't, but it'll evolve until he's a hundred. People in good health look so beautiful, even when their faces are disfigured. But the beauty of the sick only lasts three or four days.

But what's the point in proving that idea from *The Idiot*? Let's just say it's true. Because a gloriously beautiful girl just hurried past. And then I did something I had never done before in my life. I picked up the pace. Rain was falling over her blond hair. For a moment I saw a glimmer on her hair. Then the light disappeared.

It was as if the rain was seeping into a strange and fragrant sponge. And if only I could have been one of those old poets just then. If only I could have said I was the comb in her hair, and the kohl around her eyes, and a slave to a lock of hair . . . but having said all this, allow me one last confession: I write bad poems. *The Rain in Your Hair.*

Then she stopped to buy a French magazine at a tobacconist's. I felt the need to speak French. I find it intolerable to even think of two Turks, or any two citizens of the Turkish Republic, speaking French together, especially in a place like Beyoğlu. Sometimes I even find it revolting and rude. Nevertheless, I began in French:

"Don't turn around. I only want to talk to you. Don't turn around and look at me. Think of a man who has had a few glasses of beer. He wants to say something to a complete stranger, someone he has suddenly found incredibly beautiful. Keep this in mind as you listen. If you turn around you'll be disappointed. You'll say I'm a fool. You'll take one look at my dirty raincoat and this miserable hat and you'll mock me. But imagine my face without turning around. Indeed, you might even put me in a suit made by the tailor of your choice. Then maybe I'll look like one of those characters in the movies, and there's no harm in that – I find them beautiful from time to time."

I stopped for a minute. Or what I mean to say is, I couldn't go on. We both kept walking. First she seemed about to turn around and look at me. I couldn't see her face. But I sensed she was smiling and that she had suddenly made the decision not to turn around. I slowed down a little. The rain was pelting down now. I started again:

"I just threw together what I was going to say. But now I can't remember anything, and since you're not turning around I'll say whatever comes to mind. It's like this: I love a girl. She looks like you, or maybe not. But that's not the point. She doesn't love me at all. But that's not the point either. Who could I find to talk to in this rain? Who would listen? Everyone's buried in their papers, or drinking rakı at a table with friends. Everyone has something to say. But who'll sit and listen to me? And if someone did, I'd only feel ashamed the next day after having confessed everything. But I could tell you everything: how I love her and how she doesn't love me. You'll never see my face. We wouldn't even recognize each other if we met again. You're the most beautiful friend this rain could have given me. Now I'm not even thinking of my lover. Your friendship is enough. But don't take this as a declaration of love! No! I'm just telling you how I feel. But then again, I don't want you to think you aren't worthy of someone's love. You're more beautiful than she is, more beautiful than the rain. Pretending to listen to me like this is true friendship and devotion.

"You know the kind of man who follows women around and tries to chat them up. It just doesn't work – well, sometimes, perhaps. But not for me. I'm not a man like that. I've never done such a thing in my life. Maybe ten years from now, on another rainy day, I'll have four or five glasses of beer, and I'll make the same mistake."

She slowed down, and seemed confused. I felt even more self-conscious.

"Sweet mademoiselle, you should forgive even a man who follows a woman around. He has something to say, or maybe, like me, he has nothing to say; he has followed a strange and beautiful creature only to say that he has nothing to say. That's what I have to say, little mademoiselle!" And here I threw in a line right from Baudelaire, "'The world is beautiful despite it all.' Oh what beautiful rain! Oh what a beautiful lover! The pain of her not loving me smarts. But it smacks of something special. Drunkenness rattles you, makes you feel alive. What beautiful rain. Oh, it's icy cold!

And you're so beautiful: this tender girl who listened to me in the rain. I love you as much as I love her. What a world!"

Then in Turkish:

"Damn, what a world!"

Suddenly she quickened her step, and, in front of an apartment building in Taksim, she raised her hand and waved without turning her head. And, slipping through the front door, she was gone.

I was as happy as a child shaking a tambourine for the first time.

Loneliness

. . .

For the past half an hour I've heard nothing but the buzz of a fly. Oh, but the dolphins are passing by. Oh! If nothing else, the dolphins are passing by . . .

I am there as I write these lines. But when was it? I should have explained this before, before painting the landscape . . .

It came to mind only after I had penned the first sentence. It was four in the afternoon – before me sit Yassı and Sivri. If I were a little younger, if a dear friend had turned to me and said, "Come on, let's swim across," I'd have jumped into the water without a second thought – the islands are that close. I'm sitting on a rock, tickled by the chill of the sea. I'm so close. Just a little stretch and I'd be touching the water with my foot. There is a thin and sparkling line traveling toward me from the shores of Yassı to a point just 300 meters ahead (more or less). The sun hangs directly over it. I watch it race toward its end point; I watch it slowly burning away in the open space.

I was about to choose the word "tract" for "open space." But I could never figure out just where to use it. The poor word! Why should I blame you? It's not your fault. My wretched poems are still in my mind:

The tract, ah the tract
I will look into the tract
The colored cataract in your eyes

Will you die for it? Kill for it?

Rocks are all around me. I spy a fledgling seagull – the young ones have dark feathers and dark beaks. He trundles past with purpose in his stride. He knows what's for dinner, but still he's as mournful as a civil servant coming home from work. A fly is swirling around me. What are flies doing on this part of the island? Can't they find the way to that dirty butcher in the little village down the road from here? Only today he jacked up his price of his meat to one hundred seventy-five *kuruş* . . .

Beyond the bright line of light I told you about is a dark blue line. It can take you as far as the Bozburun Peninsula. My big toe is pointing right at it.

Once a painter – a friend of mine – gave us a short lesson, and while we were painting he said, "First you need to paint the landscape, and then you add the extra details." But in a story – as we prepare to paint the landscape . . . ah, there goes a rowboat – it just doesn't work. There are two people inside that boat. I can't tell who they are. They're speaking Greek. "Ah, that's Sait," one says. My dog is with me. What a pain! He never leaves me alone, follows me everywhere. He's on a rock a little farther along. They must have realized it was me when they saw him.

The weather on Bozburun looks much the same, only a little heavier, a little darker. The hills rise slowly into the sky. Sometimes I can just dimly make out a bare strip of land, or maybe a little smoke or a field of vegetables. The sea is darker here, but I wouldn't say it was windier because there's no wind today, just a little nip in the air. The piece of land that stretches to the tip of the rock ahead of me turns a little darker, like the darkening air above it; with the sudden swiftness of lace it disappears. On the stretch of sea that meets the land, two white sailboats – one fading into the blackness, and the other a little closer – but now they slip behind the rocks and are gone. And now they are back. They're tacking back and forth in ten-meter swerves off the rocks on the shore. Further along, another small hill. Two dark green pine trees with tiny emerald pine cones as fragile as little toys. To my left, a sliver of the moon. Lighting up the face of the moon in a way that makes me wonder if I'm still in this world. So bright that when I take off my glasses it almost snuffs me out. "Now what will happen if we add all this to our scene," I wonder. On my right, I can see smoke over Sivriada two knots out – to use a captain's lingo. I stand up to watch a ferryboat pass, because a rock has blocked the view. But what does this mean for us? For you it means nothing at all. For me, it's the same.

Nothing's beautiful without people. It's people who bring beauty into a landscape. But as I sit inside this moment, this beautiful September day, with the moon in the sky and the sun shimmering in the distance, like a crystal garden . . . there's no beauty. Just a void. It's just a landscape, silent and badly painted . . .

No, I'm not talking about my love. With my love at my side, this would be a paradise even God could not create. But it would be beautiful with others, too. This place is teeming with people on Sunday. The wind ripples through the Greek girls' dresses, sending them up in the air. You'll see thin-faced children lifting their arms up and throwing themselves over into the sea. The sun burns my skin. The air tickles my chest. The water licks my legs. Hayırsız Islands, Bozburun Peninsula, smoke over the mountains, sailboats, and the moon, rocks, and those green pines playing on my eyes. They mean nothing, until I can people them. So I sit here, thinking about people – and especially you, my love. Without people, without you, there is no meaning. I'm in love, that's why.

The rowboat I mentioned earlier has turned around. It's closer now. I recognize the people inside. They've spotted my dog. If they come by once more, I'll say, "Come on over, let's have a smoke." We hardly know each other, but what's the problem with that? For the last half hour I've only heard the buzz of a fly. But the dolphins are swimming by. Oh, if nothing else, the dolphins are swimming by.

TRANSLATORS' AFTERWORD

In 1925 Sait Faik was expelled, along with forty other students, from one of Istanbul's prestigious secondary schools for planting a needle in their teacher's seat cushion (the instructor of Arabic reportedly leapt up out of his chair, screaming, when the bodkin pierced his buttocks), and Sait Faik was promptly sent to a school in Bursa, a leafy city at the foot of Mt. Uludağ, where he spent much of his time alone in the school garden, pensive and withdrawn. Soon he showed a talent for writing stories – they seemed to race right out from under his pen. They were depictions of the people and the world around him, sketched in an intimate, creative, dramatic new voice. Sait Faik seemed to have the knack to sum up an entire world in just two pages. First he wrote "The Silk Handkerchief" and "The Hairspring," now two of his most famous stories. Today they are tender memories in the shared Turkish consciousness. He was an original, who wrote as he spoke, celebrating the beauty of the ordinary even as he painted in its cracks and shadows, its silences and secrets. By the time of his death he was one of the best-loved writers in Turkey.

More than half a century later, Sait Faik remains an iconic figure. The nation's most prestigious short story award carries his name. In the collective memory, he is the embodiment of the humble artist, an ambassador for the forgotten and the downtrodden. Mention his name and you'll no doubt in response get a line from one of his stories or an anecdote: how he used to send his dog to the local store with a shopping list and a basket, for example. People remember him as an honest man, openhearted, committed to his art, self-critical, unpretentious, and generous (he bequeathed his entire estate to the Darüşşafaka Foundation, which runs a school for orphans and disadvantaged children). He wrote from the gut, or in his words, "balancing on one foot," dashing off stories under pine trees, in rundown coffeehouses or late at night after his mother had gone to bed. His later stories in particular are impressionistic, surreal, hallucinatory. The selected stories here are presented chronologically, roughly following the years they were first published. There is darkness in them all, but in his last stories, there is also the anguish of a man who knows he is dying too young, and too soon.

Born in 1906, Sait Faik witnessed the First World War, the demise of the Ottoman Empire, and the founding of a zealously westernizing Republic. These radical political changes were keenly felt and dramatically reflected in Istanbul's literary circles, with alliances forever changing, and fine wars of words at each turn, but Sait Faik seemed to float above the fray, honing his own approach to writing, drawing on influences both in Turkey and abroad, always fixed on artistic integrity. At the height of the Language Revolution, instigated by Ataturk to cleanse Turkish of Persian and Arabic influence, writers were under relentless pressure to conform. But in the late 1940s, a new literary movement, the Garip or First New Movement, called for a language that was lighter, brighter and less reverent. Sait Faik was a devotee. And so his prose is an odd (and to us, bewitching) blend of the lyrical and a rough vernacular. To do it justice in translation, we often favored mood over meaning, searching for the melody or rhythm to capture an elusive phrase.

First we would choose a story, one that resonated for some reason or another. One of us would draw up a first draft and wing it off to the other. There would follow a long, leisurely, collaborative back and forth as we consolidated ideas, fine-tuning the lilt and tenor in the new idiom, settling on the right rhythm of a phrase, tracking the story to its final form. In some of the livelier poetic passages, it was easy to get stuck, and it was always helpful to run them through countless revisions with each other, shaking down the original passage over and over again for new flecks of gold.

Many of the stories in this collection first came to our attention during conversations with Turkish friends. We would list the names of the stories we had already chosen, and they would cry, "But what about 'The Boy on the Tünel'?" Or: "Don't tell me you're leaving out 'The Serpent in Alemdağ'!" We quickly learned that Sait Faik was not only a masterful short story writer – he was a dear friend to his devoted readers. Though his stories are often opaque, fragmentary and oddly plotted, they never fail to conjure up a mood that lingers in your mind for days. They are fleeting meditations, blurred pictures full of explosive creativity; intimate portraits, odes to beloved individuals or avatars (Barba Antimos, Yani Usta and Papaz Efendi); slices of everyday life, a casual remembrance, a crystallized childhood memory, a veiled and deeply personal confession. Sait Faik depicted the lives of lovers, deviants, idlers and the working class: fishermen, builders, off-the-wall philosophers, penniless widows, lost souls pocketing dreams in old countryside coffeehouses. His writing was never rooted in a fixed set of ideas; rather, his stories are stills of life organically unfolding.

Today, he risks being swamped by nostalgia. For the Istanbul he described – the city of a million souls, where, despite the ravages of politics, Greeks, Armenians, Jews and Muslims continued to live side by side in noisy and exuberant peace – is no longer. The further it recedes into the past, the greater the temptation to find in his stories the bitter sweetness of lost innocence. But as we read our way through his collected works, we came to the view that even his most charming tales had dark and troubling, silent and painfully *knowing* souls. And then there were the ones lit only – and only intermittently – by a six-watt bulb. The nostalgia hunter might find little to admire in these glimpses into violence, cruelty and perversion, but when we set them alongside their better-behaved cousins, we came to understand that there is a point in almost every story when he pulls the carpet out from underneath our feet, throws open the curtains to reveal the truth for which we are least prepared.

For most of his life, Sait Faik lived in an opulent family villa – a grand, four-story, wooden Ottoman mansion (now the Sait Faik Museum) not far from the pier on Burgazada, one of the quieter Prince's islands, where he took shelter from the crowd and wrote. Life for him was idling with the local fishermen and tradesmen on the island, exploring its quiet corners with his dogs, and, every now and then, jumping on a ferry to booze until the sun came up with other writers in the bars of Beyoğlu. Few islanders ever knew he was an accomplished writer until the day he died. Now a monstrous statue of him stands in the center of the main square, a strange twist of fate considering one of his last stories, "I Can't Go into Town," in which, on his deathbed, he remembers with a pang of nostalgia the familiars on the island and their crazy stories. Now it seems he's condemned to stand there for time eternal. Sait Faik died of cirrhosis when he was just forty-six; it was the same disease that took Ataturk, the father of modern Turkey – both had a wild passion for *rakı*, the national drink also known as lion's milk, and no doubt the lifestyle that came with it.

In his poem, "Letter II," Sait Faik writes about the great Süleymaniye Mosque in Istanbul; for him, it is forever bound up with his memories of a Greek girl he once loved. It is by weaving them together in words that he captures the essence of his beloved city: the idea that these monuments gain meaning only in the intimate stories we can share on common ground. As we bid our guide farewell, after three years of following in his footsteps from ferryboat to coffeehouse, stopping along the way to admire the birds and the violets, the gardens and the fountains, we would like to thank him for illuminating our Istanbul with his.

Alexander Dawe and Maureen Freely

GLOSSARY

Ağa: a landlord; also used to address a man of status or power

Balgami: chalcedony, a semitransparent or translucent quartz

Bedesten: a covered bazaar

Beyefendi: esteemed gentleman

Bohça: a bundle made of rough cloth

Çüpra: a more colloquial term for bream

δεν είναι: "isn't it" in Greek vernacular

Dramaduna: also Tramontana; northern wind

Dülger: john dory, a fish native to the eastern Atlantic and Mediterranean

Efendi: sir, master or lord

Efendim: sir; literally "my lord"

Eskici: a peddler of old clothes and furniture

Günbatısı: western wind

Gündoğusu: easterly wind

Han: a former Ottoman inn; many today still remain as they were hundreds of
    years ago

Haram: an action, thought, food etc. forbidden by the tenets of Islam

Hasapiko: A Greek folk dance; literally the "butcher's dance"

Helva: a sweet dish made of semolina and flour

Kalinikta: "goodnight" in Greek

Karayel: northwest wind; the mistral

Keşişleme: southeasterly wind

Kuruş: a cent of a Turkish lira

Külhanbeyi: a hoodlum or ruffian with a unique way of dressing; historically a young man who tended the fires of a Turkish hamam

Lodos: a southern wind

Maestro: Northwestern wind

Mastika: a type of rakı made with mastic

Mavrodaphne: a black wine grape indigenous to Northern Greece

Meyhane: a Turkish tavern

Meze: an appetizer usually made with olive oil

Panaya mou: Mother Mary

Poyraz: a northern wind; Boreas, the Latin God of the north wind

Sakız rakı: rakı made with mastic; mastika in Turkish

Salep: a hot drink made with milk and orchard roots, traditionally served in winter

Simit: a ring-shaped pretzel covered in sesame seeds; also a life-buoy

Sinağrit: sea bream

Suma: the grape pomace used to make rakı

Tünel: a short, one-stop funicular in Beyoğlu, Istanbul

Usta: master or artisan; also used as a term of affection

Viresi: "Hey you" in Greek vernacular

Yassı and Sivri: two smaller uninhabited islands in the Marmara Sea, part of the archipelago known as the Princes' Islands

archipelago books
is a not-for-profit literary press devoted to
promoting cross-cultural exchange through innovative
classic and contemporary international literature
www.archipelagobooks.org